Hidden Latitudes

A

NOVEL

BY

Alison Anderson

SCRIBNER

SCRIBNER
1230 Avenue of the Americas
New York, NY 10020

SCRIBNER and design are trademarks of Simon & Schuster Inc.

Designed by Jenny Dossin
Set in Adobe Electra

Manufactured in the United States of America
1 3 5 7 9 10 8 6 4 2

Library of Congress Cataloging-in-Publication Data
Anderson, Alison.
Hidden latitudes : a novel / by Alison Anderson.
p. cm.
1. Americans—Travel—South Pacific Ocean—Fiction.
2. Sailing—South Pacific Ocean—Fiction.
3. Earhart, Amelia, 1897–1937—Fiction. I. Title.
PS3551.N354H53   1996
813'.54—dc20   95-52937
CIP
ISBN 0-684-82282-2

Excerpt from "Putting to Sea" from The Blue Estuaries: Poems 1923–1968 by Louise Bogan.
Copyright © 1968 by Louise Bogan.
Reprinted by permission of Farrar, Straus & Giroux, Inc.

To my husband Alan and my daughter Amelia,

and to *Little Bit*, for getting us there.

Bend to the chart, in the extinguished night
Mariners! Make way slowly; stay from sleep;
That we may have short respite from such light.

And learn, with joy, the gulf, the vast, the deep.

— Louise Bogan, "Putting to Sea"

You do yet taste
Some subtleties o' th' isle, that will not let you
Believe things certain.

— *The Tempest*

HIDDEN LATITUDES

I dream that I am flying again, in the Electra. Beneath me are islands—not these flat desolate atolls but great mountainous islands steaming green in the heat until a fine green haze hangs on the sky to make the tired voyager plaintive with desire.

I cannot land; wherever I look, there is thick jungle, impenetrable, inhospitable. Nowhere for my three wheels to sit down, and I keep on flying. The islands never stop—on and on they bead their way across the ocean, enticing, resplendent against the blue-black water; on and on I fly, in my carapace of hot metal. I am weak with longing for their greenery, their alluring coolness of shade.

As long as I remain aloft I am free from pain and memory. Nothing can harm me. Yet I want so badly to land, with such yearning, physical yearning, that the choice is cruel. And the islands never end, they shimmer like jewels against the throat of the earth.

On I fly, condemned.

I can see a white sail on the horizon.

There have not been many, these forty years; they stay out there on the intangible line where sea meets sky, well away from the dangers of reef and atoll. They continue on their way, to Tarawa or Butaritari, or further still, to Fiji or the Solomons; no one calls at this unnamed island.

So I continue, alone.

I could light a fire and hope to divert the sailboat; there was a time, briefly, when Fred was with me, when we did light such fires and hope for rescue. But no rescuers ever came—the boats and ships did not see us, or thought we were native fishermen; they had no reason to come. Now I wonder if rescue would still be worth it; I have been gone too long. And the reef is dangerous.

I come to the lagoon to bathe at twilight each day, quickly, for there are sharks. They know me now, and respect me; perhaps I could stay longer, but I will take no chances—even now, the instinct is strong. I have been a survivor these forty years; I no longer tempt fate.

As I watch and wait for nightfall, the small sail grows larger. This is new. I sit with my back against my favorite palm tree and the sun rolls orange towards its berth. I can see the hull of the boat now, and that she has two masts. I watch as she tacks through the trade winds and grows larger as the sun grows crimson.

This is entertainment to me—I, who once had the world, literally, at my feet, now savor the slow, steady approach of a sailboat. Not, as I said, because I hope for rescue, but because there is a living painting before me now. White sails, curved like plumes to cull the wind; the familiar sun newly splendid in sudden contrast to the tiny sailboat; the plain of ocean ridden by white horses. My mind pauses on each detail, each spot of color, each contour, storing them up for the future, when my world will once again be an endless expanse of air and water, broken only by a few palm trees, some sand, some coral—my home, my shelter from the trades.

It is nearly dark; I am hungry. Usually I have eaten my supper of crab and coconut by now. Usually I have crawled into my little shelter to sleep and dream. But the sailboat still approaches. I can see a flag, I can see movement on deck—people. I hear voices; tensely, they shout and plead. A man and a woman. If they are coming into the lagoon, they must hurry, it will soon be dark and the pass is narrow.

The man is climbing the rigging to watch the reef. He shouts to the woman below; she is piloting the boat, as once I piloted the plane.

The tropical night is upon us. Light is gone; only a pale triangle of sailcloth stands against the darkness out there by the reef, as the woman tries to bring her boat through the pass. I hear more shouts, then cries filled with an anguish familiar to me only in the cries of seabirds. I am afraid they will find me like this, so I return to my shelter.

For many hours I cannot sleep. I speak to the stars; they tell me about the boat on the reef.

*T*his sky, thought Lucy, is impossibly blue. So dark it suggests the infinity of the universe, so deep that it weighs with all its heat upon a tired ocean. No wind disturbs its blueness, so we lie motionless in this sphere of blue—blue above, blue below.

Beneath her the bunk was sticky with sweat. She lay with no clothes on, because there was no one to see her but Robin, and because it was cooler. Sometimes. Now it was so hot that even buckets of water hauled in from over the side of the boat could not cool them. Hot in the sky, hot in the ocean.

Four days. Four days without wind or engine. Caught in a web of heat two hundred miles out of Fanning, growing tired and irate and wondering for the thousandth time why they were on a 35-foot sailboat in the middle of the Pacific Ocean.

She remembered her last day in the classroom, when she had given out prizes and words of encouragement, when she had wiped a few secret tears of regret. We'll miss you, they had said; she missed them now—the feverish exchange of ideas, the satisfaction of knowing she had reached them. They had given her a compact but complete volume of Shakespeare. If they could see her now: hot and naked and her hair unwashed for the last ten days. Mrs. Hughes, always so cool, so poised.

The sailboat rolled from side to side in the swell, shaking and banging with each lurching return. Sometimes the motion would stop for ten seconds or so on a freak plateau of wave, and the sensation was like that of flying, pure suspension, liberation. Then the sideways motion would begin again. Everything rattled and vibrated—plates, cutlery, things hidden deep in drawers and lockers. Sometimes it took them fifteen minutes to locate the source of an irritating noise. Everything was difficult—cooking, eating, standing, sleeping.

The engine had quit four days before, in a fit of coughing and vile smoke. They had not worried—they had sails, after all—but in all that time no wind had come to relieve them. Tension grew, as heat and thirst rose; water supplies dwindled, conversation ceased. Robin had said he could not fix the engine in these conditions; she had told him he should try. He had tried, briefly, to please her, and failed. He blamed her, he said he had only made things worse. She shrugged and, instead of commiseration, offered him sarcasm. "Can't you use any of your scientific formulas on the engine?" He withdrew into a silence broken only by an occasional oath, when he spilled his drink or banged his head during a particularly violent lurch.

Ten years, thought Lucy. You live with someone, *marry* him, you think you'd know him after ten years. But you don't. We've grown apart, not together; in moments of crisis we fail to understand each other. It doesn't *work*, we lose our temper, we lose each other.

Slow crisis, though, that's what it was. Moving slowly through viscous time towards disaster. They would run out of food and water and drift towards death not speaking to each other.

Robin sat in the shade of the flapping jib. He was fishing, to pass the time, to get away from the oppressive heat of the cabin and Lucy's bad temper. He could not concentrate on his fishing, however, and doubted there were fish in so deep a stretch of ocean. Fathomless, was the word, only it was wrong; fathomful would be more accurate, if such a word existed. But words were Lucy's domain; he had taught science. He had learned, however, since they started on this long journey, that there were many things better explained by the mystery and idiosyncrasy of words than by facts. Fathomless.

He had staked so much on this trip. All their money, their jobs, their youth and their future—all for this unwieldy, expensive, even dangerous and, so some say, foolhardy flight from responsibility and reality. But to them it meant that, like the rare flies that escape the web, they could break free of the spun illusions of middle-class life: home, car, television, bank account, jobs whose non-financial meaningfulness had long ago worn thin. Why *this* dream, friends asked, puzzled; because we will be free, they answered. Palm trees, Gauguin, crystal lagoons, that sort of thing. Solitude and finding oneself; a different and, they hoped, simpler way of life.

But it was not simpler, because they were finding themselves reduced to two personalities at odds with Nature, with each other, ultimately with themselves. Storms tested them, proved them, brought them momentarily closer, but it was the lulls which weathered them, the terrible calms when they had no words and their silence echoed the vast emptiness of ocean. Robin turned to Lucy in the night, asking for comfort, for entertainment, for solace; she turned away—it's too hot, I don't feel like it. He was puzzled by this; in their busy land-bound life she had been as happy and eager as he had, when there was time. Now there was always time, and so little desire.

Then there was the baby. They were no longer young; their life on the boat made them deceptively youthful, brown and fit, but they had entered their middle years and were learning the meaning of regret. Lucy had not wanted to stop teaching to have a child—she was devoted to "her kids," as she called them. There had been no time, anyway; they had been too busy for the better part of their life together—working to buy the boat, then finance the trip. She was grateful for the support of those excuses—sufficiently valid, however superficial—for she had to admit to herself that her real reasons for not wanting a child lay far deeper. Reasons that were not rational: a physical fear of childbirth, a psychological fear of motherhood, of being bound and sacrificed to the notions of family and society. Of being prisoner to her body and a child's demands. It never occurred to her that it might be otherwise; her own mother had been unhappy, somehow thwarted, and

Lucy had been a lonely child. Now she championed the idea—individually, not ideologically—that a woman must find fulfillment outside motherhood, that motherhood led to a form of self-oppression.

These things Robin knew, because she had explained them to him, carefully and gently. Several times in recent years he had taken her hand, and as he rubbed it, exploring her skin as a sculptor might, he heard himself promising her that with their child it would be different—he would make it different. His own desire for fatherhood was in direct proportion to her reluctance to become a mother; totally irrational as well, when, logically, Lucy was right. They had no time, and the demands of shipboard life allowed little room for babies and toddlers. They had to choose. But his desire clung fast; he had a plan. They could have a baby when they got to Australia, and spend some time there, working, until the baby was past toddler age, when they could continue on their way around the world. Children raised on boats were known to be sharp, self-reliant and imaginative. Both Robin and Lucy had seen enough of land-bound children to be aware of the deleterious effects of television, poor schools and peer pressure.

But Lucy's stubborn reluctance when Robin broached his plan to her, one moonlit evening before they left Hawaii, merely hardened into a firm resolve. Stop making assumptions about my body, she had barked. Robin was crushed. He spoke no more of children, and looked away when the rosy limbs of tourist infants wriggled in greeting—everywhere they went, it seemed.

Now she punished him with her refusal to lend him her body. Yet she was protected, there was no excuse.

Fathomless.

She moved to the sink to pour a warm glass of water. Water was rationed; she would have to sacrifice her evening tea. In this heat, she didn't care. She needed it now.

She looked out through the companionway. Afternoon length-ened the shadow of the lifeless sails, but it was no cooler. Robin was at the bow, fishing.

Fishing. Ignoring me. Doing nothing to get us out of here. Happy as a clam, and just about as talkative.

With the back of her hand she wiped the sweat from the small of her back. Once she would have thought it was sexy; now she just thought it was hot, and inconvenient, and uncomfortable. And unfeminine—though femininity had little, if no, place on a sailboat, she had discovered.

She paused to look at her face in the mirror before returning to her towel on the berth. Her long hair, pulled back in a braid, was streaked gold from the sun, which had also left little white creases all around her eyes, like miniature sun's rays themselves. She was brown and healthy, at her peak, in a blessed state of liberation from the need to please men. She was reaching an age where such things no longer mattered, where women could find again some of the anonymity and sexlessness of childhood. She had chosen a way of life where she would be sheltered from the more frivolous pressures of society. Why, then, did she care what she looked like; why did her body feel so pointless, so detached?

She picked up a worn spiral notebook and stared vacantly at a blank lined page. Lucy wanted to be a writer, in the wide-eyed way of many students, and teachers, of literature; on this trip, she reasoned, she would have time to begin. But up to now, whenever she had gone off watch and picked up her pen, either she found she was too tired, or Robin called to her to bring him a cup of tea, or she had to work on the navigation. Under way she would not have time unless it was during periods of pointless, irritating drifting; at anchor they were constantly working, repairing, maintaining, or so-cializing, or fetching water and diesel in great heavy jerricans, or traipsing around hot dusty towns in search of the cheapest, freshest vegetables. Cruising, as it was known among sailors, was hardly as leisurely or pleasurable as the word implied; it was often more tiring and time-consuming than land-bound labor.

But when she did have time to pick up her notebook, her inclination was to fill the pages with criticism and complaint. Her focus was not the disinterested, exalted release of creativity; rather, her words competed with one another for the most accurate description of her mood, and she took a grim triumph in seeing herself reflected on paper. This was not writing after all, she concluded, but was unable to break away from her own reflection. She was surrounded by a mirrored surface of ocean.

Behind Robin, the jib snapped, then bellied, hesitantly. He looked up. The sea's oily surface was now brushed with a darker, rougher patch, moving towards them; the jib again snapped and filled, the boat responded. Where had the wind come from? For so long it had seemed impossible that they should move again, yet now the breeze was upon them, invisible, mysterious. He pulled in his fishing line and ran aft, to set the sails, and a course.

Lucy dozed. When she awoke the boat had found her true motion, her smooth, effortless obedience to the wind. It was like flying; they had come thousands of miles like this, but in four days one could forget. She went out on deck and joined Robin in the cockpit. The light had changed with the passage of the sun, glowing copper now on the white sails and their own skin. At such times they forgot everything, and needed no words; a smile sufficed.

After supper they stood over the chart table. They would have to head for Tarawa in the newly independent republic of Kiribati, where the harbor at Betio might have facilities for the repair of the diesel. But Robin was reluctant to take the boat into the lagoon without an engine—there would be more traffic there, and it might prove a tricky entrance. On their course was the small island of Marakei; he suggested stopping there in its sheltered lagoon, to try to repair the engine first. Lucy agreed happily; she did not care where they went, provided the engine could be repaired. Lucy did not particularly like, or trust, engines. They bored her. Sails she could understand, and handle (without getting dirty), and repair. Sails were about poetry ("the wind's song and the white sail's shaking") and grace, and discovering continents, and being at one with Nature. But being of her era, she could not deny the importance of the engine, when approaching port, when there was an emergency. And when they were becalmed.

They sailed all day and through the night. By late afternoon they could see what they thought was Marakei—a mere ripple on the western horizon, a barely discernible irregularity on the smooth geometry of the Pacific. Lucy took the sextant up on deck and, after working out the sight, confirmed their position on course for Marakei.

This sun sight would later be the source of much bewilderment and accusatory questioning (But are you sure? A running fix? What about the dead reckoning? the index error? the timepiece? How could it be nearly *eighty miles out?*) Anything was possible with celestial navigation; all you could do was aim your sextant at the sun and drop its orb onto the horizon, then follow all the rules, fill in your worksheet with your figures, check, double-check . . . Robin and Lucy on their yacht *Stowaway* followed all those rules, but in their haste and anxiety an error must have been made. They would never know just what put them so far out that day.

By dusk they had rounded the southern tip of the atoll and were swinging north-northeast towards the pass as it figured on the chart. They worked their way back and forth across the wind to approach the entrance. They would need skill and a steady wind to take the boat through the pass almost at an angle; they would need to keep a sharp lookout for the reef.

"I'll go up the rigging now," he called, giving her the wheel, and with his binoculars around his neck he climbed, agile, monkeylike, up the ratlines.

"What can you see?" she called.

He gestured, an impatient thrust of his free arm to the right; she turned the boat slightly to starboard.

The round, not quite focused, image in his vision soared and dipped with the motion of the boat; now sky, darkening quickly in the tropical nightfall; now the ocean, black to deep turquoise where it fringed the atoll; now the waving unbroken chorus line of palm trees. He looked for the pass, glimpsed the lurking darkness of the reef, then to his right saw a blurred lighter patch; he blinked, looked again, confirmed, waved to the right, ignored Lucy's questions, stopped to rest, clinging, breathing; the sweat was running off his back. Then he looked again, hesitated, began to gesture, and broke off.

It is so dark, already; Lucy at the wheel, her eyes sharp on the approaching island, squints at the movement of the waves— breakers on the reef; a hint of something beyond the lagoon, a seabird? Then she looks above her, to her husband, dark against the taut whiteness of sail. He is shouting, his words lost in the wind, his arm madly gesticulating, now to port, now to starboard, now straight ahead. "Where's the pass?" she calls, suddenly frightened; she squints ahead, where there is a wall of white water, she swings the wheel to port, then to starboard, looking for a break in the wall. Robin is shouting, both arms now clinging to the shrouds; she cries out, turns the wheel hard about, but it is too late. The awful cracking lurch, more sensation than sound, tells her they are on the reef.

I did not sleep well. I worried about the sailboat by the reef—were they able to find the pass? It is so narrow, I hardly know it is there myself. When I had the old raft I used to explore the lagoon. The pass is an initiation, of departure or arrival—to the wide sea, or to the small enclosed world of the island.

I go to the lagoon. Close in by the shore is the sailboat, quiet, unmoving. So they are safe; they have been lucky indeed. Perhaps they are asleep in the stillness of the morning. Of course, they come from that other place, beyond the ocean; they will not have the habits of the island, of rising with first light. And they are tired, they have traveled.

I used to travel—how I traveled! The most-traveled woman on earth—I nearly circled the globe. Only one small ribbon of ocean remained to close the circle, from here to Hawaii. But I saw too little, learned even less, and took with me only postcards of experience from those places I touched—and a desire to return, some-day. Mere names on a map, some of them, viewed only from high above, but I can still recite the names, their poetry: Qala-en Hahl, Umm Shinayshin, Idd el Bashir, Marabia Abu Fas . . .

But I wander. What of my tired visitors? How am I to greet them? If I greet them . . . They must be European or American, that seems obvious from the neatness, the modern cast of their vessel. Will they remember me or even know me? What language do they speak?

I sit in the early-morning shade and eat my breakfast—banana, papaya, coconut—and watch the sleeping sailboat. Tiny crabs scatter at my feet. Usually I play with them, but today there is something much more interesting to observe.

*

People. I open my mouth and speak the word aloud: "Peo-ple." It rings strangely in the still air here by the equator, one little word shot out in such a wilderness. I laugh, then think better of it. I do not want to alert them to my presence, not yet, at least. Until I decide.

I have been here so long. I have seen almost no one, since Fred. There were those who brought fear and forced me to hide; and then there was the gentle islander—but that, too, was long ago.

People, I whisper. Then, man, woman, sailboat. I speak to myself all the time, but hearing no answer, I no longer hear myself. Now that there is the possibility of an answer, I say, and hear, those words, and they ring with exotic promise, like Idd el Bashir, Marabia Abu Fas.

*I*t is difficult to rise, to face the day; they lie silent in their berth, holding each other, as if that is all there is left to do.

There is no repealing the sudden interruption of time, when they knew something awful had happened; there is no remedy for the knowledge that nothing would ever be the same. There has been a destruction of faith, a loss of innocence, from the moment of contact between the coral and their wooden hull. Lucy screamed; Robin more fell than climbed down the rigging. The rest has become a blur of gestures and impressions, unreal in mere memory. The boat heeling awkwardly to one side as the waves pounded against her, as greater waves of panic rushed upon them. The mainsail, lowered in haste, flapping like a ghostly shroud against the darkening sky. The life raft, the life jackets, the eerie light of a flare against the darker dusk, a moment of apocalypse in their simple lives. They clung to each other, pulled away, cried, oh no, oh God; one of them put out a Mayday on the radio, unanswered.

Then the flood of dazed relief as they found no water gushing into the boat. The bilges were almost empty—they had not rammed a hole but were stuck fast. There followed the trembling wait, which seemed so long. But it must have been brief enough to spare the boat from the surf's destructive pounding; they would never know, in terms of seconds and minutes. They only knew the awful groaning and shifting of the unhappy boat as she bumped and settled with the waves. Would the tide rise and carry them off, or would they be forced to abandon ship before the surf smashed the *Stowaway* to pieces?

Slowly, as the wind dropped, as the moon rose, the boat rose too. They had been spared, the moon showed them, at the very edge of the pass: a few more feet to port and they would have lost the boat; a few feet to starboard and they would have made it through, frightened but with innocence preserved.

They tossed the dinghy over the rail; Robin's heart pounded as he leaped into the pitching craft, already awash with waves. Somehow they managed to fit the outboard onto its bracket; he would not forget Lucy's frightened face as she passed the heavy motor down to him, so afraid she would drop it, her hair blowing in front of her eyes, hiding her tears. Somehow he managed to get the outboard started, and the moment *Stowaway* lifted free, he gunned the engine, pulling the heavy boat away from the reef and across the lagoon, to this safe, still anchorage. The moment of crossing was unreal; the moon shone like a cinema projector onto a fantasy, a nightmare of worst fears.

I wait a long time by the lagoon. The sun climbs and the heat pours down from the crest of the palm trees. There is a figure on the deck of the sailboat. I move to hide behind a tree, for shade, for safety.

Now there are two figures. The man, the woman. A few hundred yards away. He is tall and fair and bearded and wears an odd-looking pair of shorts. She is small and stands by him, hesitant. I watch as they move about the deck. They are preparing to set off in a small rubber boat tied alongside the sailboat—it is not unlike the raft we came here with. The man climbs over the edge of the sailboat and steps into the wobbling dinghy; she passes some things to him. He sits and puts some large goggles on, then flips himself backward off the edge of the boat and into the water. I consider warning them about the sharks, but then it would be all over for me. She is there to watch, and they will learn quickly enough, as I did.

He disappears under the boat for thirty seconds or more; she waits, one hand against the rigging as she watches. Then he surfaces, and holds on to the side of the boat for support. Their words travel in the still, clear air—the first music of the human voice I have heard in many years. It takes me a moment to realize that they are speaking English, and that I am actually able to understand them.

"It looks bad," he is saying. "It's hard to tell how deep it is. There's a huge gash where the plank got stove in, and a long scrape—it must be where we got stuck." He shakes his head from side to side; even from afar I can read the dejection on his face. They look at each other across the short distance; there is something familiar to me about that look, that moment of shared hopelessness, when courage or faith have slipped away and one looks to the other in astonishment, for help. I remember those moments, among the others.

"Oh, Robin. Will you be able to fix it?" she asks.

"Lucy, it's not something I can fix, like an engine or a broken toy; it's almost an organic part of the boat. I don't know, I don't know how bad it really is, how much it has weakened the structure." So his name is Robin, and she is Lucy; named, they will find their place in my story. There is a pause as he looks up at her; she is unhappy, wiping her hand against her eyes. Then he continues, more gently, "We'll mix up some underwater filler, to protect the wood, at least. But I'll need to make up a backing plate to strengthen the plank where it got stove in—maybe try to push it back out. We can't sail with it as it is now, it seems fragile, too vulnerable. But we can do something for now, until we can get to Betio to replace the plank. We won't lose the boat. Okay? Isn't that good news at least?"

I cannot hear her reply; he climbs into the small boat and she joins him. What happens next makes my old heart contract within me.

She puts her arms around his neck; he turns to her and kisses her. The kiss is slow; she clings to him, now kissing, now burrowing her face in his neck. He wipes her cheek with his thumb, and they kiss again.

I cannot say I had forgotten—oh no, never forgotten. The kisses still haunt me as I lie awake, bound by stars. But they are dead—ghosts, like those I loved; insubstantial, as I reach out into the night air. The death of my kisses was the death of all kisses. But now I see that I have been wrong, that there is life, still throbbing, out there beyond the lagoon, beyond the wall of ocean. There are still kisses. How can I live with that knowledge and accept my captivity?

But there is no time to think about that now. The small boat is coming towards me, towards the strip of sand below the trees. My instinct is to hide, and I follow it—it is both too soon and too late to be discovered.

*

I retreat to my shelter, to its shade and protection. No one has ever found me here, so artfully does the shelter blend into the small hot landscape of coconut palm and pandanus tree. Fred and I built it; over the years I have replaced the worn palm leaves, carefully weaving the fronds together to make the shelter as dry and protected as possible, though this is sometimes difficult in the winter gales. But it has withstood heat and storms and intruders alike, and now it must withstand kisses.

An unfamiliar weakness has come over me. Voices, language, touch. They are the very age I was—

Don't think. Don't. Such thoughts bring sadness to press upon the island like a reproach. The island is beautiful in its clarity and simplicity, it is not at fault. It has loved me, in its way; looked after me. Given me a great, unusual gift.

I breathe deeply and smile. My secret is truly a secret now that I have someone to hide from.

They are here, walking about the island.

*R*obin walks ahead into the trees, his step confident, comfortable in exploration. Lucy hangs back and he has to wait for her. The heat makes her listless and she has a fear of the unknown. There is no one here, she thinks, and although they have crossed thousands of miles of ocean alone, there is a disturbing obscenity to this solitude. Land is meant to be inhabited, she thinks, even atolls in the Pacific Ocean. There should be the huts of itinerant fishermen, some mark that the island has been colonized, made human. She does not know why this expectation should make her feel better, but it does, and she looks around in anticipation. The island breathes silently in response.

Robin waits for her. "What do you think? Our own desert island?"

The cliché depresses her, but she smiles. "Perhaps it isn't deserted."

"What makes you say that?"

She pauses, then, "Surely there's a fish camp, a tiny native village, no?"

He shrugs.

"Besides," she continues, "on the chart it looked like there might be a village."

He is thoughtful for a moment, then says, "I'm not sure we are where we thought we were."

"What do you mean?"

"While you slept I double-checked the navigation . . . I don't think this is Marakei. It doesn't even look like Marakei. It's too small."

"What? What else could it be? There were no other islands anywhere near our position—"

"I know that too, unless . . . It is a very old chart."

Lucy pauses and looks out beyond the spotted shade, beyond the grove of coconut palms to the bright boundary of ocean. Not where they thought they were? Lost in the ocean?

"Also," he says, looking down, "there was an error in the sight reduction. Not a lot, but enough to put us out sixty miles or so, maybe more." He looks at her, wearing his teacher's smile of gentle reprobation.

"So where are we?" She flaps her arms in exasperation.

"Latitude two degrees thirty-six minutes north, longitude one-seven-four ten east. Give or take, as always."

"And is there an island on the chart?"

He shakes his head.

"Then *your* navigation must be wrong—the timepiece, the index error, something—"

He shrugs and looks away. "I didn't take another sight," he says. "I only corrected yours."

"Well, does it matter?" she exclaims, suddenly angry, eager to argue, to hold him responsible for her anxiety. "It's the flipping wilderness, wherever we are! We're not about to find a boatyard here, are we, with a diesel mechanic and a shipwright—we're stuck in some godforsaken wilderness!"

He draws her towards him, not in a real embrace, for it is very hot, but in a gesture of conciliation. "No, my love, it doesn't matter. We're here. We didn't lose the boat—that's what matters. Nature was kind to us—God, was she kind!" He hurries on, eager to forget the night on the reef, to dispel the shame of their terror. "We have food and water, and a radio, and some wood and underwater putty, and an engine manual, and a lovely, deserted tropical island to shelter us for a few days."

She nods and returns his gesture, but still feels uneasy. It is not just the island, this uninterrupted procession of coconut palms; it's not even not knowing where they are. It is being dependent upon Robin to get them out of there . . . This lack of faith is more disquieting than her sense of dependency. Why does she not trust him more, why can she not place herself, childlike, in his charge? She watches his strong brown back as he walks ahead of her, and sees him, angrily, as her only means of survival. If anything should happen to him—a bite, an infection, food poisoning—

A breeze greets them, a sign that they are nearing the windward side of the island.

The island embraces its lagoon, like a crescent moon curved perfectly around its shadowed self. Lucy and Robin walk its length and breadth, but see no sign of human life, or even any indication that life as they know it can be sustained. They see few plants other than the ubiquitous pandanus and coconut palm; they find no water. Once, they are startled by a thud in the trees behind them and Lucy grabs Robin's arm. "Coconuts," he reassures her. "They fall out of the trees when they're ripe. Watch your head."

Robin reckons the island to be two miles in length and perhaps half a mile in width—a poor island, neglected, insignificant, unworthy even of tourism. There are no hills, no valleys, no rocks; only the bright unchanging purity of sand and coral, the undulation of the palm trees. And there is the heat, pregnant with moisture like the false promise of rain; it seems to Lucy that the full weight of the cloudless sky is upon her, making movement, even breathing, a struggle against some invisible force.

The heat follows them back to the boat. They lie exhausted in the steaming cabin, relieved only by the occasional passage of breeze through the hatch. The fears of the night before ride in and out of their drowsiness like the breeze; never have they been so uneasy with life or so aware of its potential for tragedy. They cling to the safety of the lagoon, yet fear it, too.

Lucy gets up and goes to the ship's radio.

"Calling any vessel, calling any vessel, position two degrees thirty-six minutes north, one hundred seventy-four degrees ten minutes east, do you hear me? Please come in . . . calling any vessel, calling—"

"You're wasting your time," Robin calls.

She clicks the transmit button off and looks over to where he lies.

"Why?"

"No one can hear you."

"There might be a *ship*—"

"Look, love, we're not in any danger, I told you. What could anyone do—tow us to Tarawa, or Honolulu maybe? Or perhaps you'd rather abandon the *Stowaway* here, an appropriate graveyard to our dreams?"

"But they could help us, they might have engine parts, at least tell us where we are."

"We don't need to know where we are. We just need to eat and sleep and fix the plank and the engine so we can get away from here, all right? Have faith, give me a chance, please, Lucy."

She replaces the radio transmitter in its cradle, but leaves the radio switched on. Just in case. She needs to know if there is anyone out there. She needs to know that they are not alone.

Robin surrenders to heat and heads for the forward berth for a siesta; Lucy sits by the ship's radio, brooding on its silence. She picks up a crossword book, gets stuck on "quasi-stellar radio source," and puts it down; she deals out several hands of patience and loses miserably. Now and again, from Robin, a faint grunt or sigh. He sleeps with the purposefulness of a man who has a job to do. She knows he would prefer for her to be in there with him— despite the heat, despite their nervous fatigue. He would reach for her, she would be his reassurance, his moment of oblivion in their time of difficulty. At the same time, however, he would disregard her anxiety and her need for a different kind of reassurance. She wants action: an arm around her shoulders, his own voice booming down the radio. Sex is powerless against this anxiety, this brooding impatience with the present.

Besides, sex has become a problem—an awkwardness, both

physical and emotional. Small boats are not sexy; cramped, rolling berths require ingenuity and patience. Lucy feels she has neither—she wants the space to roll towards, then away, to indulge languor. Emotionally, shipboard sex has become a chore, a service to be rendered among so many others. She blames the boat, then wonders if it is not the natural evolution of their marriage.

She goes to sit up on deck as the air begins to cool. The lagoon is calm behind its retaining wall of breakers; beyond, the sea is flecked with whitecaps. The sun is low. She looks towards the island; it lies serene and silent in the muted sunlight. Even in this caramel, domestic light the island seems hostile to her. Not because it is, but because nothing in her experience has prepared her to deal with its wilderness.

She places her palm upon the still-warm teak of the deck, feels its smooth grain and the hot ridges of black caulking. So solid, so safe, after all. Despite the reef. How many boats survive such encounters? She blocks her thoughts against the horror of the night before, accepting the accompanying thud in the pit of her stomach as proof enough of their narrow escape from something darker and more horrid still than the reef and its churning breakers. Strong, strong boat; she touches the wood for reassurance, for luck.

Robin awakes at dusk and returns to his workbench. He has begun fashioning a support plate to reinforce the damaged plank. The work gives him some satisfaction. For although he does not know if the boat will be strong enough, should they encounter bad weather on their way to Betio, he knows he is bound to do what he can, in order to regain both his confidence in the boat and his wife's trust.

He carries the piece of wood with him to the main cabin. A locker under the port berth has been cleared of its contents to reveal the damage. Stout old boat, he thinks, not for the first time, as he looks at the cracked, slightly buckled plank trying its best to keep the ocean out. To someone who does not know the boat as Robin does, the damage is hardly visible, but he can see it, and wonders if it can be measured against the strength of the ocean. Water is seeping in, mercifully slowly, but Robin has no doubt that it will get worse. The boat's wound is somehow fascinating to him—the quarter inch of newly exposed wood, the seeping seawater, the suggestion that this fragility could still sink the boat, and their dream with it.

He works quickly, measuring, cleaning, covering the surface with sealant. Easy to fix, in a way, he thinks; if only wounds to the human heart were as simple to repair. He is worried about Lucy. Since they struck the reef she has distanced herself from him in a new and strange way, as if she did not know how to deal with this unexpected hardship. As if it were his fault, or as if she could no longer accept the more apparent risks of this oceangoing life. It was never her idea, she has gone along with it for his sake, happily building her nest when it comes time to provision but often reluctant to stand watch or do routine maintenance work. She's your baby, she has said once or twice, with cruel thoughtlessness. He always wants to reply, If you'd give me a real baby we wouldn't be here now, but the subject has become one of those unapproachable sources of strife in a marriage, and now Robin holds his tongue.

He can hear her in the galley making dinner, her clipped gestures full of reproach. He pauses to listen. He cannot understand her anger. Is he not fixing the plank? Did he not pull the boat off the reef? Will he not also fix the engine, then sail them safely to Betio? Is that not enough?

But perhaps in this modern life love can no longer be measured in traditional terms of devotion and sacrifice, of protection and caring; perhaps the rules have changed. Robin does not feel heroic—although he would like to—because she does not see him as heroic.

He returns to his work. The wood is ready: a few holes to drill and then the plate will go in, a perfect fit, a strong, if temporary, barrier against the unthinkable.

They eat quickly, in near silence, then Robin finishes his work on the plank while Lucy clears away and washes up. When his work is done he calls to her to come and take a look, and she smiles approvingly as he shines the light against the wood. A certain relief is visible on her strained features. It might, he suggests hopefully, even push the plank out flush with the others again, which might in turn lessen the seeping. As he speaks and explains he realizes he is hoping for a parallel improvement in their relationship.

But Lucy goes to bed almost immediately and sleeps heavily, defiantly, leaving Robin alone in his wakefulness to listen to the sound of the breakers pounding in the distance against the reef.

I awake to the early call of birds and remember—the man Robin, the woman Lucy, the sailboat. They have repairs to do, they will be here for some time. I will be able to observe them, to learn the ways of society once more; then, when I am no longer afraid, I will be able to choose, to stay or to go, to continue here or return to the ways of society.

But if I choose to go, I will lose the gift of the island.

What does it mean to them, to be lost here on this tiny scrap of earth pretending to be land, this unmoving ship on a too-large ocean? They, at least, can leave again; their ship with its wonderful white sails can carry them wherever they plan to go, to those who are waiting for them, family or friends.

We once had the whole world waiting, but we sailed with the brashness of an era. We were testing the mastery of our time, staking our lives on the best, the most advanced, that men's dreams could produce. The best was not good enough for Fred and me, but I have seen, and wondered at, the great trailing ribbons of cloud in the sky above me. So it continues, the quest; others succeed where I—we—failed.

Every night in the clamoring refrain of receding memory I hear the question: Would we have made it, if we had kept going? The heavy cloud outside the windshield, Fred's scribbled notes, passed along with the fishing pole we used to communicate from his space behind the fuel tanks to the cockpit; no celestial sight possible. The vibration of the cockpit, the fuel gauges dancing before my eyes, the numbers in my confused head, so tired, so far to go . . . How much farther? How much time? How little fuel?

How little fuel, how little time.

And the radio, I hear it too, the silence or the crackling speechless static, and my own voice pleading for *something*, some recognition—Yes, you're there, we see you, we hear you, steer seventy-five, steer one hundred and five, you're nearly there! But there was only that silence; every night as I fall asleep and every waking dawn (it was dawn then, too) I hear that voicelessness.

Fred's note, finally, with the line of position; my own strangled voice telling the waiting ships by Howland, could they but hear and answer me, 157–337, north and south; north and south I flew, but could not see them, could not hear them, could not find them.

We turned around, while there was still time. Back to the Gilberts. Perhaps we could make it there by dawn, before the fuel . . .

Hopeful, I flew.

Hope was the only light in the midst of fear, such a tiny light against the vast darkness of ocean. Hope made me search the endless expanse below me for islands—real, living, tropical islands, not tiny military runways lost in the blue waste of the Pacific. I huddled stiff and scared over my controls, trying not to look at the treacherous gauges, trying only to see something—a beacon of land to moor my ship, a beacon of hope.

Then the fuel gauge, the final cough of the engines, the realization that hope was powerless to delay the moment; now I could hear Fred shouting from behind the empty tanks, but I could not hear his words, despite the sudden silence. Was it the rush of air against the fuselage? Was it the pounding of blood in my ears? The falling altimeter, the terrible unfamiliar sound of our gradual descent, the approaching insubstantial runway of water, the rising wave of panic, the final note from Fred: Preparing Life Raft, Have Faith.

There is a dark veil over those few seconds before impact, a refusal to remember, a blankness, a fragment of the oblivion I had courted. Fred later told me, perhaps in jest, that it was the best landing I'd ever made. I could only believe him. A clean, level landing, like a fist in a cushion, braked by a great spray of water.

We were afloat. I had bumped my head; I looked through the glass at the ocean as into an aquarium. I sat for a long time, it seemed. As if waiting for ground crew to run up to me. Fred's hand on my shoulder. I can still feel it. We had to survive, it said, so many words in that touch.

I lie here now and, forty-odd years on, it is as vivid as yesterday. I have lived on my memories, after all; I have read them over and over like books unworn by time, unchanged because my perspective so rarely changes.

It was a brief, last triumph, not the one we'd expected, not like the ones I'd had before — Burry Port, Londonderry, Oakland — but the one that could have been so different and was so different for the wide unknowing world. There to greet us, after the long westward drift from the sinking Electra, was no wall of reporters and photographers and well-wishers but a waving crowd of palm trees at the edge of a tiny, oh so substantial island. We cried, we laughed, as the surf tumbled us onto the beach; we did not know if we could survive there, but we were on land again after thirty hours — only thirty? — of air and ocean, and the very fact that we were alive and could be safe for a moment was enough. We looked at each other and cried with joy, we flung our arms around each other, danced a mad jig by water's edge, hugged the palm trees, then lay beached, exhausted, on the cool white sand, at dusk.

I often go to that windward beach and look to the east. I can see certain things. The Electra's tail as she bade farewell, sinking, sinking; a ship on the horizon; cities hovering, ethereal towers; great white whales; gathering, advancing armies. And I see myself and Fred, clearly, as on film, as we were that day in our funny round rubber life raft when we first saw land, when despair turned to joy. I have, since that day, known greater joy, and greater despair. Nothing can move me, I am safe.

*

We found water, a small spring in the northwest corner of the island, near my present shelter. We knew we would live. Fish were plentiful—the trick was catching them. We were loath to use the hooks and line provided with the life raft—it was all we had, and we had to know we could make something else if we were to survive on fish for any length of time. Fred said he would make a spear. In the meantime there were coconuts; there, too, we had our difficulties in opening them at first, until Fred was able to whittle a spike from a strong piece of driftwood.

All we had in the world was in the life raft: my suitcase, with a knife I'd bought in Batavia, a few shirts, slacks, a change of shoes, an overall, a thin raincoat, a few toiletries. Only the knife seemed of any importance. Fred had rescued some clothes and a small metal box containing a few pencils, a cigarette lighter and cigarettes (which he soon finished), a picture of Bea, his wife of four months, and a hip flask of Scotch. We had our log, all the paper we could carry; only a few navigation books. We had no Bible, no Shakespeare, only the almanac for 1937! I berated him—why had he thrown these things into the raft and then forgotten the sextant?

He told me he had not forgotten it, but simply had not had time to get it. He had grabbed what was at hand. In his experience of sinking ships the main thing was to get off in time.

I see him in the shade of the palm-leaf shelter, bare-chested, wearing torn-off trousers, poring over the navigation tables. He tried so hard, with his watch and sticks in the sun and scratchings in the sand, to compute our position. He was sure we were in the Gilberts, to the northeast of Marakei Island.

I only found out years later: he was absolutely right.

How he struggled against his beard. He tried to shave with the knife. At first he made huge gashes in his chin. He had no razor because he had not taken his overnight kit; he was sure we would be rescued.

We saw the planes. And a ship, the one which is always there when I gaze out to that place from which we came. Everyone had told me not to worry if we went down in the ocean, that the Electra would float because of her empty fuel tanks, that she would be visible like a huge scar on the skin of the sea and help them to find us. They were wrong. She barely floated long enough for us to climb out of the upended rear hatch and get off with the life raft.

With a precious bit of fuel from Fred's lighter we started a bonfire, in hopes that they would see the smoke by day or the flames by night. For days we tended the fire, thinking they would return and see us; for days we ate coconut and grew thin and learned the bitterness of waiting, like death-sentenced prisoners hoping for clemency. Then the planes stopped passing, and we knew they had given up.

We were no more. The aviator and her navigator who had tried to circle the earth had ceased to exist, vanished into the clouds. Swallowed by the sea, they must have said, and say still.

We had to learn to redefine ourselves, our reduced world, our shattered expectations. We could no longer expect to be rescued, and the island—welcoming enough as a temporary and beautiful wilderness before our supposed return to a relieved world—was suddenly hostile, as if it did not want us to be there either.

The heat made us irritable. Until the planes stopped coming, Fred and I had worked as a team, overcoming past differences in our need to survive; now we knew we would survive, but only in forced captivity on the island. We argued and shouted and raged about trivial things. Sometimes he stalked off into the bush, as he called it, and stayed away for two days or more. His absence was both a relief and a terrible, lonely apprehension.

We could not continue to eat only coconuts. But the lagoon, we discovered, harbored sharks, so we hesitated to fish, even once Fred had managed to fashion a kind of harpoon. One day we'd had an argument about something pointless from our pre-island existence and Fred grew so angry that he waded out into the lagoon, water up to his waist; he began to wave the harpoon above his head, shouting, "Come and get me, confounded sharks! Finish me off! I don't care, I'm done for in this godforsaken place. Let the famous aviator get out of here if she wants—she's got wings, let her fly!"

He waited a long time, alone in the turquoise water. His chest heaved with anger, with the effort of shouting. Finally one lone creature appeared, indolent and only vaguely menacing. It circled slowly, sizing him up—was he worth the bother, such a skinny, meatless specimen? Fred watched, now silent, his spear poised. I believe he would have speared the shark, wrestled with it single-handed—to survive, or die fighting? But the beast turned with casual disdain and glided away.

Fred caught five big fish that night; we cooked one and hung the others in strips to dry.

After that Fred fished and I kept shark watch.

We became dependent upon each other—not in an open, reasonable way; it was begrudged. Not in the old way either, with me piloting and Fred shooting the stars—that had been professional. Now we had to look to each other like two children lost in the woods.

There was loneliness. Family and friends had given us up for dead, and we could no longer place our hope in them. They had died, as effectively as we had.

In those early days we stepped away from ourselves and lived like strangers to our own souls. We gave each other so much of anger, of despair. I accused him, wrongly, of bad navigation; he accused me of flying extravagantly, full throttle, not monitoring the fuel. Loneliness blossomed wildly under the tropical sun, bursting into a poisonous defense against the other person. He called me a prima donna who'd never done a real day's work in her life (how unfair, how little he knew me); I called him a drunken Irish womanizer. Those were our old roles, our old prejudices; we did not see the real person through the veil of despair which separated us.

Now I see him clearly, sitting in the sand, his head in his hands; he rocks gently back and forth. "Oh," he chants, "for a shot of whiskey"; we had finished the contents of the hip flask by the second day.

This sailboat, out there, in the lagoon . . . they'll have everything. Bread and butter and jam, soup and canned meat and maybe even Coca-Cola, maybe even Fred's whiskey—

He made things, on good days. Whatever bits of wood he could find he sculpted, more and more skillfully as time went on. Some of it was merely decorative—sharks, dolphins, fish, airplanes—but some was useful and helped us. Spoons and bowls and plates; small dull knives and rough combs. He made another spear and some remarkably strong fish hooks; he even made some water jugs out of the thicker pieces of timber that washed up.

I watched and felt stupid. I still have those things, I keep them by me in the shelter. I play with them, like a child, and act out stories; like a child I know the delights of invention and imagination.

I learned to walk up and down the island and came to know it intimately. I wrote books in my head, full of rambling philosophy and melancholy poetry, but I could never bring myself to put any of it onto paper. The paper had to be shared, so we used it for silly things, in the end: ticktacktoe, battleships . . . We erased until there were no more erasers; by then the paper was thin and fragile. So I wrote my poems on the island, memorizing, assigning the first line to the first tree, the second to a mound of sand, the third to a clump of undergrowth, and so on. Sometimes Nature would change and lines of poetry would be lost. Always I would come around to the spit of land's end by the lagoon, to where my existence was thrown back upon itself in the cool reflection of the water, to where the poem would end.

What, in those early days, did we expect? Of course in our way we silently, separately, kept hoping—for a ship, for islanders. We would look at each other and know we were alive and the presence of the other kept us from madness. But our lives were apart and our great loneliness untouched. We still saw ourselves as the famous aviator and her navigator; we had not let go of the outside world's image of us, and if a newspaper crew had suddenly fallen from the sky onto our island they would have found nothing changed between us.

We did not touch. We were very proper, circumspect with each other. Our shelter was small, but we lay apart, each thinking, no doubt, of his and her respective spouse.

There was never any question—

Oh, for those lost months, those early precious days of lonely, distant companionship, still in the bright sunshine, pure and new and strong. All those minutes and hours and days, lost, spent, gone forever, that could have been so much more—

Oh, for those lost months.

*T*t is their second day on the island, and they wake early, alarmed by calm and isolation. Lucy smiles to Robin, sorry, now that it is daylight, that she was so distant in the night; Robin, mindful that she is merely positioning for power and trying to forestall his mood, ignores her. He cannot deal with petty emotions now; there is work to do.

After breakfast he prepares to dive under the boat to patch up the gashes caused by the coral. He calls to Lucy, who is waiting on deck, and asks her to mix up another batch of putty.

At first she watches as he works his way under the hull in the glass-green water, but then he disappears, and her gaze lifts to the horizon, searching, searching. She almost misses the movement in the foreground: it is just a flash, a gray streak of motion. But she knows, from popular legend as well as atavistic instinct, that this is danger. She pulls frantically on the rope Robin has slung beneath the hull to provide support while he works. He surfaces, breathes, directs an irritated grimace at her.

"What is it, what's the matter?"

"Get in the dinghy—oh, quickly, don't look, just hurry!"

Robin obeys, too slowly and precisely, as if to underscore his irritation with her panic; once in the dinghy he turns and looks behind him. He says nothing, merely nods to the retreating fin fifty yards away.

Lucy's face is brave yet tearful, her lips pressed in hard against the surge of fear within. He takes her hand, but cannot meet her eyes with his.

"Do you have to put this putty on?" she pleads. "I mean, don't you think the risk of going into the water—"

"If I don't get under there to seal the wood, the risk of worms eating the hull will be far greater than the risk of the shark eating me. Not to mention the water seeping through and possibly weak-

ening the plank still further. You just keep a good watch and tug if
he gets as close as before, right? Now mix that putty."

She watches anxiously as he dives again, with his spatula and
little palette of putty in one hand. The shark has moved off and is
well out near the reef; Lucy cannot estimate the danger, in shark
matters. She looks down at the putty—two jars of goop, one black
and one yellow, which must be mixed in equal parts to make the
wonder putty which will save the boat. She hesitates. Robin mixed
them using first the spatula, then his fingers. He has taken the
spatula with him, but it looked easy enough, like making pie
dough. A watchful eye on the shark, Lucy dips her fingers into the
black goop, wipes a wad onto a board, then dips her other hand
into the yellow. "Everything okay?" shouts Robin as he comes up
for air. "Fine," she calls, checking the shark. She looks down
again at her putty, then plunges her fingers into the black-and-
yellow dough on the board.

After a moment she cannot believe what is happening, and looks
around for assistance from some unknown quarter. With each
thrust of her hand, more putty leaves the board to cling to her fingers in a gluelike vise, until a lump the size of a large apple is
hanging from her hands. The more she pulls, the more it sticks, until there is virtually no putty left on the board at all. Yet it remains
tenaciously black-and-yellow, which means its chemical usefulness
has not been reached; it must turn a shade of gray-green, like vomit,
to work. Disbelief turns to anger; now she is pulling, stabbing, jab-
bing, tugging; tears well in her eyes. Damned boat, damned reef,
damned husband. She is crying in earnest now, tears tickling cheeks
she cannot scratch. It is as if the entire welter of ordinary hurt and
frustration accumulated during her marriage has been made
tangible—black for hurt, yellow for frustration—and would destroy
all touch, all sensitivity.

By the reef, the shark has turned and is laying a direct course
for the *Stowaway*. Lucy shouts, she cries, she tugs on the rope with

her bare toes. Robin surfaces and turns, and mutters, "Shit," very quietly. He could reach the shark in three or four laps, but it is the shark which will get him first. Other arms than his own seem to propel him into the dinghy and safety just as the shark pauses. Do sharks think, or sense? Robin wonders; why has it stopped? Fascinated, he watches as the animal veers away again with a graceful, insolent twist of its horrid body.

Patiently, as if he were soothing a child, Robin removes the putty from her fingers, deftly neutralizing it with salt water. "Never mind," he says. "Don't worry, I'll mix the stuff up myself, no repair job on earth is worth seeing you so unhappy."

He puts his arm around her and kisses her cheek. "Better?" She nods. His arm is cool from the lagoon. Her cheek is warm, wet and salty. "Go below," he orders gently. "Cool off for a bit."

"And the shark?"

"I'll wait. You calm down."

Even her anger. She cannot have her anger. He defuses it, turns it to guilt, makes her feel childish. Turns legitimate tears of distress into a child's calculated whimpering.

She goes to the wine rack, where there is an unopened bottle of tequila. She tears the seal and unscrews the top, and takes a deep long swig. It burns and confuses her briefly, then leaves her with a supreme, burning isolation, detached and aloof.

She returns to her shark watch. Robin dives, patches, surfaces, mixes putty, dives again, back and forth for an hour. The shark has disappeared and he is able to finish the job undisturbed.

In the late afternoon Robin begins work on the engine and Lucy decides to row ashore. He looks at her, concerned; he looks at the row of palm trees that suddenly, in his aroused imagination, might hide secret dangers, as the lagoon hid the shark. Lucy insists she will be all right; it is too hot on the boat, and he will be making such a mess, with tools and engine parts all over the cabin sole, that she will not be able to move around. Besides, she needs some time away.

Lucy looks regretfully into the clear water as she rows across to shore—it would be so refreshing, there would be so much to explore in that turquoise world. She feels dispossessed; her established notions of where she belongs or is tolerated on earth and in Nature have been upset. The open ocean gives her a grudging right of passage; but now the coastal waters where she has always felt welcome to swim and dive are hostile, and land offers none of the usual, human, reassurances. It should not be like this, she reasons, we should be part of Nature and feel that we have our place anywhere on earth. Yet Nature does fail us, because we no longer know her, because we abuse her; we have lost our communication, our interdependence. Not only that, but there are people who would rather live, by choice, in the most crowded, urbanized of cities—New York, Mexico City, London—and who can exist, quite normally, quite comfortably, with a minimum of trees, water and open sky. She is not thinking of poor people who have no choice; she knows students, teachers, intellectuals, artists, who never leave the city, whose entire landscape is man-made, airless, confined. How can they stand it?

She pulls the dinghy up onto the beach and pauses in the shade to catch her breath. They stand it, she thinks, because their true, important landscape is with each other, verdant with shared ideas and beliefs, lush with the fruit of culture, history, art . . . This idea, as she walks towards the eastern shore, through the green-gold thickness of trees, suddenly depresses her—she has always believed in Nature as something necessary and vital, but now she realizes that a part of her, undernourished, is beginning to atrophy in the wilderness they have chosen. She misses the city, civilization, being part of a great cultural connectedness. Her spirit is no longer lively with ideas and expectations, challenged and growing.

Yet if she were in the city, would she not be longing for precisely this—the peace, the solitude, the tropical paradise? Is there not an entire industry based on the exploitation of people's frustrations and on the absurdity of workaday lives made meaningful by two-week budget holidays? But of course such paradises are often replications of city life: crowds, high-rise hotels, organized leisure, rampant consumerism in the form of useless souvenirs—illusions, carefully packaged and marketed.

She looks around her and tries, for a moment, to picture this island wilderness peopled with ice-cream vendors, time-share hawkers, middle-aged matrons and their large-bellied pink-faced husbands; or the lagoon cluttered with flotillas of sailboats, their crews congregating over six-packs and pot-luck dinners. The island, imagined thus, becomes friendlier, safer, infinitely more familiar, however far from "unspoiled" it may be. But Lucy then imagines herself disappearing into an oppressive, overwhelming crowd; she becomes anonymous and insignificant in such a landscape.

She reaches the eastern shore of the island and faces the ocean she has crossed, beyond which is all she has known of the world, a place to which she will, someday, return. The wind is there, gentle and cooling; she finds shells at her feet, pink and ivory and the palest of gray. She kneels to pick them up, to touch the glassy smoothness of their interior, the ribbed intricacy of their exterior. She marvels at the craftsmanship which knows no craftsman.

The island begins to whisper to her, an entreaty, or a promise. It will give its simple beauty to her, freely; it offers her a place. Something fills her, unexpectedly: a great, bright awareness, a thrill of knowledge, a pure, physical understanding. She sits by the shore and lets the feeling surge over her to the rhythm of the waves, until she has melted into the dusk-deepened light, cleansed, serene, changed. She knows this is only the beginning, she knows the island is entering her life.

$\mathcal{T}$he girl is here. I observe her from one of my hiding places. She sits facing the east, as I often do—that is where the trades come from, where we come from.

She picks up shells and turns them over in her hands, choosing the ones she likes most and putting them away in the pockets of her shorts. She pauses and breathes deeply, head thrown back, eyes closed. She likes it here.

It took me a long time to like it here. It was long after Fred was gone—some weeks after the intruders from the west had sailed away and I was sure that they would not return—that I surrendered to the island. I began by naming everything here. I had to, like the early explorers of the New World. I could not live here and be forever a stranger to the island and its creatures, to its wild vegetation. So I made up names, absurd but perhaps more appropriate than the real names—which I shall never know. A small darting bird became a flibbertigibbet; there were scooter crabs and hoppity crabs, and see-through shrimp; in the lagoon there were zebra fish and steamroll flounder. The larger animals I knew, but they too must have proper names, for I learned gradually to recognize the individuals of the species. One particular dolphin I called George, affectionately, after my poor widowed husband, because he seemed to lead the others. Some of the sharks earned the names of people from my past who had been particularly hard to deal with; others were named for politicians or warmongers. Trees and flowers and bushes were named; some I knew or thought I knew, close enough; other strange tropical plants seemed to grow their own, inexplicable names: hadzawei, mandiwa, molimoli.

Places, too, must be charted, but this time there would be no naming for people, no false glory; no Vancouvers or Magellans or

Drakes. The merest mounds of sand or baylike indentations of coastline, rocky outcrops or coral formations, all were named. This is the Cove of Desolation, because you look to where you cannot return; the small elevation where I hide watching the girl is Watcher's Mount. This beach is called Bone Sands—for its color and because I once found a bone there. The lonely sandspit at the north of the island is Cape Sorrow; the hidden grove where I have my shelter is Shangri-la . . .

But I did not name the island. That naming would be too permanent, no longer a game. How does one name a universe?

From the time of the naming, the island became a gentler place. The sun no longer burned, the rains no longer pelted, food became plentiful and easy. I was able to swim whenever I wanted to and feel sheltered, buoyed by the waves; the sharks rarely troubled me. If they swam near, I swam away and walked out of the lagoon, calmly. I learned the brief tropical seasons just as my body lost its own seasons. I did not mind that early change of life. Now I could rhythm myself to the sunrise and sunset, to the moon and tides, to the rains and winter gales and summer squalls. I learned to care deeply for the clouds, to know what lay in each shifting ripeness of gray or black; I learned to welcome the rain and its gift of coolness. But there would be droughts, too, times when the clouds were relentlessly absent or were tumbled high and white and barren and I would fear for my spring.

I watch the girl and wonder what her life has been and what she knows of clouds. Does she know that this approaching darkness by the horizon announces a squall, and that she will be stranded here until it passes, unless she returns quickly to her boat?

I am drawn to her. She is, first of all, a woman, and I have not seen another woman since we left Lae, New Guinea. She could tell me so much—how we are doing in the world, how the world itself is doing. I could tell her of my life here and lighten my burden for the telling.

But I am afraid. If I reveal myself to them, the magic might end and return to the deep source of the island. I lost it once before, when the flowers failed to bloom and the clouds were barren. What would happen to my secret, to my magic relationship with time? And would the girl not lose the magic I can, now, share with her?

She is leaving. I follow her quietly through the trees to the still, dense air of the lagoon. As she rows her boat, the first sharp puffs of the squall crease the water and drive her more quickly to the sailboat. That is her small universe—her man, her home, her journey. Closed to me; I cannot follow.

I watch until dark. Small lamps are lit, the sailboat glows dimly, like a welcoming cottage in a Christmas-card snowstorm. Around me the palms begin their Balinese dance in the wind, supple and compliant. Where do I belong?

*R*obin lies restless on his bunk, defeated by mechanics. The first day of work on the recalcitrant engine has yielded no solution, has failed even to reveal the source of the problem. He thought that calm waters, rest and unlimited time would lead him to the answer, but the ways of inanimate objects are often mysterious, exposed only by trial and error. Nothing, yet, has worked; no amount of thinking, either, seems to help. He is dejected, in need of consolation, but Lucy is still on the island.

Memories lurk and beckon, uninvited. Robin lets them in, because Lucy is not there to see. As if in her presence the guilt of those memories would glow on his face like radiation, or alter his features in some way; as if she would divine from a frown or a musing smile all those events she was unaware of while he was experiencing them.

He closes his eyes and the girl is there again, her face above him a bright glow of joy in the dim shuttered room. That joy entered him, too, as if luminosity could fill one's veins and make them pulse with youth and breathless anticipation. How nothing else seemed to matter but her face and her warm lithe body; how his knowledge of her permeated the air he breathed and the words he spoke, and lent the light of an impressionist's palette to familiar streets and buildings.

Not so long ago. In the midst of their preparations this girl had come to him and stayed, so briefly, those two months and nineteen days. The headiness of those days; Lucy had thought his frantic excitement was due to their approaching departure and his final days of teaching. She did not know how he was spending all that time she thought he was working on the boat. She did not see him park several streets away from the flat of his former student, did not see how he could barely keep from running those few blocks. How proudly and defiantly he walked them, for all to see but

Lucy. He had tempted fate. He could be there still; he had very nearly called off the whole trip.

He could be there still, in the dim shuttered light of mid-afternoon, among whispers and muted laughter and the slow passage of the faint ribs of light along the wall, in a quiet pool of desire.

Robin remembers and stirs with an uneasy tingling sensation, of desire and regret. He gave her up for this, his dream, his planned, careful dream, which included a wife and a child and a journey halfway round the world from that room, from that fulcrum of his life, discovered too late. His wife sulks and avoids him, his child is nothing more than a plea, his journey is fraught with danger. He thought he had made the noble choice, to stay with Lucy, to continue to build on what they had. There had never been any real doubt in his mind, any other real choice.

But now in this lagoon he is tired and spent, and very lonely. It is hot, not warm; the sky through the porthole is a circle of black approaching squall. He closes his eyes and lets the girl's face hover some minutes more above him; her long hair encloses their kisses like a veil.

That is how Lucy finds him. Sleep hovers, Robin frowns and purses his lips. She sits down on the opposite berth and looks at him for some minutes.

She felt so alone on the island—yet not lonely. As if she were part of something, as if she belonged, even briefly. But often, of late, she feels lonely with Robin. His mind is elsewhere, not just in trying to understand engines. Their fears, instead of bringing them together, seem to deepen the rift between them.

Robin smiles in his sleep. How like a child is a sleeping man, beard and all, she thinks. Innocence regained. She feels a momentary surge of tenderness, then checks it. She suspects he is not innocent, that there is a struggle between them for power over the other's life. She wishes that she could be free from the struggle and live with the simplicity of the island. That watching her sleeping husband would be a moment of joy, like the moment on the island, unattached and pure.

The first gust of the squall hits the lagoon and causes the boat to pitch suddenly at anchor. Lucy turns away, a knot of fear in her stomach; Robin awakes. He looks at her, severely; nodding, she follows him on deck. They check the anchor and keep watch, silently, as the squall passes, brief and spiteful like a child's tantrum. For a moment the lagoon is splattered with small waves and ripples and the island kneels to the strength of the wind; the sun is hidden behind a black smudge of cloud. Then it is past and a dark-amber light encloses the lagoon.

Such moments make it worth it, Lucy thinks. This light, rarely seen—a sign, a blessing. She wants to reach for Robin, to touch him, to feel him there. But when she turns he has gone; she sees him disappearing through the hatch. She stays on deck a moment longer, wishing she could drink the light, keep it inside her; then she follows, there is supper to prepare.

Over dinner Lucy questions Robin about the engine. He explains, glumly, that he does not really know what is wrong; it starts, then fails. He has bled the engine, tried a number of other things. She waits, letting him finish, then says, too brightly, "Well, what will we do if you cannot fix it?"

He looks at her and does not answer.

To short-circuit a conversation that would be tedious to her, and to give him a shot of self-confidence that may or may not work, she says, too glibly, "Oh, go on, you'll fix it. I know you will. You're good at these things—much better than you give yourself credit for."

Robin watches her rise and go to the forward cabin. He feels cheated. He is not "good at these things"; he has been a teacher, a mechanic of the mind, not of hard metallic things. He merely tries, and they both know it. He feels a heaviness descend upon him at her departure, her refusal to commiserate; he feels the weight of lost illusions. Lost illusions should be light as air, should evaporate and make room for others, but instead they press upon mind and heart. First there had been the freshness, the brevity of passion; and now this possibility of escape, with its dream-fulfillment urgency, shows itself to be unjustly dependent upon the strength of their marriage to sustain it. He recognizes the way in which Lucy's words did indeed land glibly upon his shoulders, only to bounce away into nothingness. Her support is not genuine, she is elsewhere, on a different course. Without her support, sails luff and slat, the boat goes nowhere. He is going nowhere. They are merely sailing from place to place, getting older, staying childless. Where are the way points, the landmarks to show them the progress they have made?

Robin thinks about the equator. A magic, invisible line in one's geography, never before crossed, hidden over the horizon a hundred miles or so farther south. They will not reach it for some time yet; they still dwell in their own familiar hemisphere with its habits of seasons and stars and water gurgling clockwise down a drain. He wonders if in his own passage through life there will be a distinct awareness of crossing a hidden latitude; or will he, like the navigator bent over charts and figures, learn of his crossing only when it is far behind him?

One can pass back over the equator, but in one's own life there is no going back over the line.

Later, in the darkness of their cabin, he reaches for her. Stars watch, unobserved, through the hatch. It is too hot, their bodies stick, then move apart in discomfort. He pictures the cool green lagoon just beyond the hull and hesitates. Do sharks ever sleep?

Probably not, or probably not now. He reaches again; her arm responds in a sleepy wave of irritation. Like brushing away a fly.

Robin turns and lies awake for a long time, his mind forming a deliberate, meticulous schematic of intricate moving parts—tiny washers, fuel lines, nuts and bolts.

I slept badly again because of the presence so near the island. I awoke and listened to the birds, as I do every morning, but I could not concentrate, could not recognize their voices or their song.

It is late. I hear an engine coughing, dying, briefly throbbing from the lagoon. I know it is the couple on the sailboat, but the engine sound fills me with a long-forgotten fear and I turn on my grass mat, arms around my ears, to fight the remembering.

A still day, many years ago. The heat heavy, pressing the sky down upon the island. I went to the cove at dusk to look for the trades, to watch the distance for planes and ships. I still did some-times, back in those early days—Fred so recently gone, the diffi-culty of living. Like the girl, I sat and watched and dreamed and looked to the east.

They were there almost before I knew it: a shout, a few hun-dred yards away up the beach to the north. I thought I was dream-ing, but in my dreams a human presence meant warmth and rescue. That shout, those running figures, five or six of them, were awful to me, and meant unthinkable things. This I knew, instinc-tively.

They were small Oriental men. They wore uniforms and their faces were very young and hard, with an insolence of youth, be-neath their cloth caps. I did not take time to see more but rushed into the ocean; I did not care what happened. It did not matter if I died in the surf, as long as I died whole, alone. I was gambling on the absurd assumption that they would either not know how to swim or not care enough about me to risk the sharks. I felt I had less to fear from the sharks than from those men. Perhaps if I dis-appeared effectively for some time in the water, they would think I had either drowned or never existed.

I swam out past the breakers. The current was very strong and I worried that I would be swept away. I could still hear them shouting, nearer now; they were Japanese, I recognized the refined staccato sibilants of their language. Still swimming, I looked back to the shore; one of them was waving a gun. There were more shouts from farther away, excited chatter, then laughter. They walked away, into the trees, to join other soldiers.

Night came, and welcome darkness. I had been in the water for at least an hour, perhaps more. The current had carried me south, almost to the end of the island, far from my shelter which, in any case, they might have discovered and destroyed. I let the waves take me ashore again and I lay for a long time on the sand, listening, fighting sleep. I could hear a low humming beneath the island's desolate music of waves and wind. I knew they must have come by ship and that their ship must be outside the lagoon, to the west.

The moon did not rise. Clouds blackened the stars. I walked cautiously to the southwestern curve of the island and looked out past the lagoon. There was the ship, a black smudge against the black night, barely lit. What did this mean? Why was a Japanese ship in British-protected waters—if I was indeed where Fred had said we were—darkened and full of soldiers?

At dawn, with some difficulty, I climbed a small coconut palm, as Fred had taught me. I clung to its tip, sheltered and hidden by the surrounding canopy of leaves. But I was almost immediately tormented by thirst and heat and I was afraid that I would fall asleep and lose my grip. I watched from my perch and waited. The ship did not leave. I could see the sun rising clearly now, from the east. They call Japan the land of the rising sun, but these soldiers had come from the west. The heat addled me as I puzzled this. Somewhere, because of some cartographer's vision of the world, my island lay lost, adrift, neither east nor west, midway between north and south, undefined, out of established notions of space and geography. I sat at the top of the palm tree and it was the top of the known world. Around me the universe spun in madness, beneath me small men scurried against the earth's gyration, heedless of geography.

On that strange morning, poised on the edge of my existence, geography lost all meaning. I thought I could see, far, far on the horizon, the other top of the world, the snowy heights of the Himalayas melting the color of apricots in the morning sun.

All day I watched from my parched aerie, as launches carried groups of men back and forth from the ship to the lagoon. At times their laughter reached me, at other times I thought I heard cries of protest. I slept in brief fits of vivid dreams, red and black and full of fear. In the afternoon I heard awful inhuman cries, then gunshots. At dusk I crawled down from my tree, taking a coconut with me. I was stiff in every muscle, weak, dehydrated. Without my stake it was very difficult to open the coconut. I banged it against the coral, cutting my hands, shattering the nut and losing its water. I had to tear the meat with my teeth. A drop of blood left a perfect red sphere upon the white flesh.

Through the night I waited and the ship did not leave. Perhaps they would never leave. I had dug myself a bed in the sand behind a mound. I felt as if I were already buried alive, half-dead from fear and exposure on an island made hostile by man. At dawn I was woken by more shots, but there were no cries. I slept again, exhausted. They might have found me there, half-buried, only my madly dreaming mind still alive, still caring.

The heat woke me and I crawled to the water's edge to cool off. I felt the sun on my back and knew it must already be high above the trees. I scooped the water over me, its blueness almost tangible as it fell upon me with the softness of petals.

When I turned he was there, watching me, absolutely silent as he smoked a cigarette. Was it because he watched me so serenely, without shouting or calling to his comrades, that I did not cry out or run or dive into the water? Although I could not read his thoughts I could study his face: young, refined, perhaps confused at being here, merely curious. I guessed, from the good cut of his uniform, that he must be an officer, and his silence and stillness were therefore his prerogative.

We stood watching each other. The waves breathed gently against the shore—in, out; the sun continued to rise and shed its heat. The officer smoked, and did not take his eyes from me. I waited, my arms around my wet shirt. The moisture began to prick my skin beneath the hot fabric. I dared not run—I saw he had a gun cased in leather against his side. I thought that I might appeal to his youth, to an attitude of respect I sensed rather than saw in his stillness, his poised watchfulness.

He finished his cigarette and shifted his weight, as if to move forward. He was crushing the cigarette in the sand and he lowered his hands, near the gun now. I could not move. Barely breathing, I continued to hold that impassive, impenetrable gaze. It came to me as smooth as his skin, as the blue-black hair beneath his cap. He swayed gently forward on his toes, like a drunken man, and his head dropped down from his shoulders until I could no longer see his eyes. Then, briskly, he spun on his toes like a dancer and strode away.

He had bowed to me.

I could not stay there. I was afraid he would return with other soldiers. I was so tired. I could not go back up the tree—that had been a mistake. I was sunburned and aching all over. I did not think I would have the strength to swim. I thought of my shelter, a palace—could I, after all, hide there? The growth was the thickest on the island, the shelter itself built thickly to blend in with the trees and undergrowth. If I could get there, I might be as safe as anywhere.

I walked quickly with a feverish lightness along the beach, looking over my shoulder in the direction of the ship. I could not see it but I could still hear the throb of engines, the occasional shout or command. I pictured the young officer. Was he, at that very moment, telling a superior about me? Would a launch return to shore to look for me? But I did not walk any faster, I just kept my stride, glancing over my shoulder, until I reached a quiet spot where I could no longer hear the throbbing, and I sank down onto the sand, mindless of the heat.

Inside me rumbled an explosion of despair—why was I there, alone, unprotected and unable to save myself, so miserable from heat and thirst? For a sick, unspeakable moment I thought of giving myself to the Japanese. Perhaps they would restore me to my own people. I did not know if we were at war; surely any fate at their hands could not be worse than this enforced captivity, this bleak prison of palm trees and dry sand with its bars of endless ocean . . . I was tired, so tired. They would feed me, clothe me, give me a real bed, a hot meal. They were human.

But there had been shots, and cries of pain . . . theirs was no mission of peace. I had come to know my island, and I knew it would let me survive.

I reached the shelter and slept until dusk, a horrible dreamless sleep interrupted by moments of wakefulness, where in my imagination I heard the soldiers' cries and more shots, where I saw them coming towards me, saw hundreds of launches in the lagoon, the entire island prostrate to the step of boots. When it was dark I got up and left the shelter. I stopped at the spring to drink, then walked on to the lagoon.

The water lay still, undisturbed, under a star-speckled sky. I could see no light where the navy ship had been, no dark smudge.

There was no sound of engines. I sat and waited until dawn, to be sure they had gone. While I waited I spoke very quietly, turning words like sweet cherries over my tongue, sending messages across the longitudes to my lost family, to Fred, to the Japanese officer. I spoke to them all and listened to my strained disused voice and I heard their answers. All the while the stars turned above me, hard and brittle, and the ocean spoke against the sand, and the trees nodded, approving.

In daylight I learned of my danger. The island lay open like a wound, alive but desecrated, violated. Above the beach by the lagoon, in the middle of the island, I found the two bodies. Already there were flies and a horrid, unfamiliar smell. I focused on those physical details to keep from thinking of that other, greater horror.

One was a young man, his skin the color of burnished mahogany, his hair dark and smooth. His flesh was soft and round where the bullet marks lay. He seemed at peace, merely asleep. I believed him to be a Gilbertese native.

The other was a white man, very pale, sunken and old. His hair was white and he had a small mustache, too quaintly dapper on a face frozen in fear. His eyes were wide and frozen pale in disbelief. His white shirt was stiff with blood. The collar had been carefully starched and pressed. I imagined someone doing that—a red-cheeked wife in a flowered apron? A round, brown servant? Someone had ironed that shirt and had not been aware of its final destination.

I walked away from the flies and the smell, but waited by the bodies. I may have prayed for them; I thought of how I might have been their friend. I thought of their families, of all those who waited, who did not know . . . A wake of a kind. There was only me to mourn them.

At nightfall I gathered all the driftwood and scrub I could find. I went to the shelter for Fred's cigarette lighter. Then I returned to the bodies. With difficulty I dragged each one down onto the beach and lay them close together. I placed the wood around them, on top of them, beneath them where I could. I did not know if this was right, but it was all I could do.

The flame caught after a few tries. The pyre burned easily. There was a great light—I was afraid that an enemy ship would come. I had not thought of this, I had only feared that smoke in the daytime would be more visible.

That night, for the first time, I heard the voice of the island. I heard it in the crackling of the fire as it burned and burned, cleansing, purifying, transforming its two victims into air and lightness. I watched and felt the fire's terrible heat and feared its brightness until it was all over; at daybreak a small, clean mound of ash remained, barely visible against the sand. How could that be? I wondered. No charred sticks, remains, nothing? Just ashes?

A breeze disturbed the small mound, briefly; behind me the lagoon rippled. I looked up: a barely perceptible movement in the palm leaves, a mere hint or shrug.

It was at that time that the magic began. I found blossoms, where before there had been none. Just by the mound of ash, in a semicircle, then all over the island, many astonishing, beautiful flowers: hibiscus, Barbados pride, cup of gold, frangipani—borne on what wind of change? The island grew fragrant, a tapestry of rich, joyful colors. I dried hibiscus flowers in the sun and placed them in a bowl of water. The tea they gave was tart and refreshing, the color of blood.

*L*ucy leaves Robin after a brief silent breakfast of crackers and raspberry jam. She has tried to gauge the level of reproach in his silence, the grunt which implies, see you later, I'll be here. She tries to qualify her own guilt. Is it because she is leaving to explore while he works? Because of last night? She rows to the beach through the star-washed water, and pulls the dinghy ashore.

She walks and the knowledge that the island is hers, her special place, becomes material. There, beneath her feet, the earth, sand and coral; beneath her hand as she passes, the ridged textured scaliness of a palm tree. The occasional querying call of a bird greets her, musical and clear. Baby's-breath clouds overhead—this is new. The heat, still oppressive, is laden with a moist salt smell.

She grows drowsy and sits in a palm grove with her back against a tree trunk. Waves of sleepiness wash over her, bringing colorful, confused visions—the island, the boat, herself and Robin. Her old fear is there—of the solitude, the imprisoning reef of coral, the circling shark. But the means to conquer her fear is also there—Robin, smiling to her and saying, have faith, I'm here, I'll get us out of this. And, stranger still, an imagined voice on the ship's radio, murmuring don't worry, you'll be all right here, what could happen, you'll be safe for as long as you stay. Come back, who are you? she cries; she starts, and awakes to disappointment. The voice is in her dream.

As she lies back still farther, her gaze shoots skyward to the splayed green-gold fingers of the palm trees, and she is enclosed, protected, lulled; but also curiously uplifted, borne closer to the veil of blue beyond the trees, to the stately traveling clouds.

After some moments she stands, shakes off sand and residue of sleep, and walks away from the lagoon to the eastern shore, to the ocean side. Where the lagoon is sheltered, dozing in a haze of baked light, here the wind raises the breakers upon submerged reef and beach, where they exhale their great long-traveled sigh of arrival. Lucy waits and watches; her senses expand and the island enters her. In colors, textures, shifting light; in waves of heat and wind; in the call and answer of bird and ocean; in the ripe dusty odors of vegetation. Until now, Lucy has known the natural world only through the critical distillation of the mind; now the island reaches for her like a lover, all warmth and abandon and ripe desire. She responds; she throws off her clothes and runs along the stretch of sand, arms outspread, hair flying, feet dancing along the laced edge of the ocean. Like a dream of flight, all lightness and joy; like love freed of the shadow of the other.

But there, wait, as she pauses to turn she sees, just ahead of her in the virgin sand by the water's edge, the slight depression, the mark, elsewhere meaningless, of human passage: a footprint. Her own? Impossible, she has not walked this far today. Approaching, she puts her foot into the indentation. Her heart is there now, pounding, reminding her of fear, of existence; her foot fits the print, but no, not perfectly, those toes are surely longer; she stamps her own impression into the sand, next to it, hard; there, it is shorter, fainter, it lacks the firmness of the other print, it cannot be hers. Are there others? She walks on, quickly, lightly, along the waterline for some fifty yards, sees none, turns back. The print is still there, unmistakably human, definite.

Her own hard-stamped print has nearly faded.

Lucy turns, grabs her clothes and runs to the lagoon.

Robin cannot understand so much fear. He knows his own, a menacing, stalking thing to be held at arm's length with all the strength he has been taught. He cannot understand the shaking, sobbing bundle in his arms. He tries to talk, to comfort and explain, but she cries and clings. "You weren't there," she insists, "I saw it, there's someone there—"

"And if there is? Did they hurt you? Perhaps they will help us.

Perhaps they're as frightened as you are. Please, Lucy, calm down."

He pours her a glass of brandy. She takes it docilely; it cauterizes the edge of her fear and brings a sudden sense of the unreal, of the irrational.

"Perhaps," he suggests, "it was your own, from another time?"

She shrugs, nods, sits up and away from him; she is making a fuss, being irresponsible. He leans and kisses her; he cannot tell her, yet, that the engine work is still not going well. It will only alarm her. He takes the radio transmitter in his hand and speaks slowly, calling unidentified vessels, any vessels; he smiles to her. Of course there is no answer, but he has tried.

That night she reaches for him, clings, draws him to her, into her. All the gestures are right; they flow on their own hunger. For once the heat and sweat add to their desire, making skin slide and taste of salt. She is, briefly, in command; he submits, barely aware of his elation. Then he lies back, sated and content, but he is uneasy with the knowledge that her need was not born of desire or harmony, but of self-preservation. She is using him as a shield against her fear. Her body can forget itself, briefly, in this uncharacteristic display of passion, but her mind, he knows, is elsewhere, behind her tightly shuttered eyelids; elsewhere—still fearing, struggling in its own private place.

Robin goes ashore early, before she awakes. He stalks the island, his eyes rove like searchlights. The air is still. He listens, but can hear only his own breathing. He walks until he knows she will miss him, and worry about him, then paddles back through the rising heat, empty-handed.

For several days Lucy does not leave the boat. She reads, plays cards, cleans, passes tools to Robin where he works in the engine room. The engine starts, once or twice, then hiccups into a coma once again. Robin sweats and swears; Lucy watches, detached, waiting.

They have been at the island for a week and Robin begins to worry about their water supply. The tanks were half-empty when they arrived, after the long passage from Fanning; they never thought they would be stranded here for so long. Robin frowns at the relentless blue sky, its occasional barren clouds. It might be another month before it rains. He decides, foolishly late, to increase the water rationing.

Lucy does not take well to this new restriction. It is further confirmation of their dilemma, of the hostility of their environment, of the failure of things to behave in a predictably human-controlled way. She too takes to watching the sky, casting the occasional angry glance towards the island. She feels it has betrayed her.

They decide to go ashore again to look for water. The island is so lush, so seductively green, it is hard to believe it cannot sustain all forms of life. They search for several hours in undergrowth and shade, then return, parched and defeated, with empty water jugs.

Lucy asks Robin to check the level of the water again, to work out how much longer they might have.

"It's not an exact science, you know," he tells her. "There's no gauge."

"But can you tell?"

"I can only compare what's there to where it was when we arrived, and to when I last checked it."

Robin looks, his head in a locker, upside down and sideways, with a flashlight shining on the side of the white plastic water tanks. A faint gray mass should indicate the amount of water remaining. He looks, shifts his body, looks at the other tank, then at the first one again, while Lucy waits, refusing to believe they could actually die of thirst.

He sits up and does not say anything.

She expects him to say the tanks are nearly empty and crosses her arms.

"Well?"

He shakes his head and lets out a short, impatient sigh. "It's funny. I would say the level has hardly changed in a week. I'm sure . . . I'm sure it's where it was when I last checked."

"Don't be silly. We've used loads."

"Well, that may be, but I know what I see. We should be fine for a while yet. Good news, no?"

She shrugs and flaps her arms. She does not trust this easy answer, this failure to question. She worries, and he brushes her worry off like a fly.

I have frightened the girl. I did not mean to; I did not mean for her to stop coming or to fear the island. There is nothing to fear on the island, nor has there been, for so long.

I saw a footprint once, too. It was some years after the Japanese had been here, and I was afraid that they had returned. A footprint on the beach by the lagoon, but no launches in the sand, no ships anchored beyond the reef. Like the girl, I went back to place my own feet in the prints, for there were several, and like her I was dismayed to find they were not my own, but were rather larger, and longer; the stride, too, more extended: most probably a man's.

I did not know what to do—hide, and miss possible rescue? Or look for the man, and hope he was not hostile? And if there were more than one?

I walked along the beach by the lagoon, to the south, and kept by the trees for cover. The sky beyond the western horizon was dark, thick with lowering hills of clouds. A squall or storm was on its way—this has always made me happy, for with it comes fresh water, to wash, to cool the air.

In the southernmost curve of the lagoon I found a small outrigger canoe with a tiny tablecloth of sail. It was old, primitive; there might not be room for two people in such a small craft. This relieved some of my fear, but also made me sad, because it meant that there might not be room for me to travel with the canoe, to such a place where canoes are made, where people live, and eat, and laugh together.

I waited and watched the clouds and the gentle bobbing of the canoe at water's edge. So long since I had seen another sign of humankind. This canoe, for all its simplicity, was made from Nature by human hand, and shone before me with all the craftsmanship and beauty of a Renaissance sculpture. I touched the strong, supple wood, I ran my fingers along the thick weave of the sailcloth. I thought of the technical complexity of my last airplanes—how they had left Nature, or even craft, so far behind, to become the offspring of technology itself, somehow beyond Nature, beyond even human touch. Those planes no longer had their place in the natural world. And yet this small craft might take me away from here, where all the Electra's engineering had failed, because the outrigger was at one with Nature, at only one remove from a dolphin or a seabird. In the design of the plane, in its very essence there had lain a fatal flaw: its dependence on fuel to stay afloat.

I marveled that I had once been part of that conspiracy against Nature. I had been on the island for so long that I knew it could sustain me, I knew it intimately and loved it for its minute, daily generosities. It was as if, having taken Fred from me, having tried, and failed, to restore me to the monstrosity of civilization with the Japanese invasion, the island had admitted defeat, repented, then embraced me. I looked at this humble canoe and understood what the islanders, through isolation and poverty, had always understood.

There was a sound and I turned. The islander stood a few steps away and looked at me without hostility, his eyes sharp and warm, his face a bright confusion of surprise. I tried to smile, not knowing what strange rictus must be contorting my face. A smile: so unpracticed, unreflected, except in thought.

He approached slowly. He was tall and palm-slender and quite young; he smiled, his teeth were very white. He stopped and made a tentative greeting, then hesitated.

"Hello," I said slowly, my voice, like the smile, cracked and rusty, so loud in my ears.

"Hello," he answered, almost a laugh; then he extended his hand, rather formally, and said in thickly accented, schoolbook-correct English, "My name is Kuma."

I told him my name, then asked him how he had come here, and from where.

He pointed to the west and said, "Abaiang," then gestured, great sweeps of his arms, and blew with a whooshing sound like the wind in a school play, concluding with peals of laughter. I understood that a storm must have blown him far to sea.

He asked in turn how I had come here. So strange to tell someone—a story from the past, so long ago, it no longer seems real, as if it had all happened to someone else and had come to me as a legend. He looked at me in disbelief, astonished at my fifteen years here. Did he understand his own importance, did he understand that he was going to take me away from here in his too-small canoe, that for fifteen years I had been waiting for him, gentle Kuma, to deliver me?

I finished my story. He gave a nod, looked at me brightly, then said, "I am hungry—have you some food?" I motioned to him to follow.

We walked through groves of palm trees and pandanus, splashed with the color of hibiscus and frangipani. After the Japanese had left, the island revealed its abundance. Had I previously not seen what was there, or not known how to see? I had discovered bananas, papaya and breadfruit, and I had learned to use the taro root; my stock of dried fish—all speared with ease in the lagoon—was varied and plentiful. I had learned to keep a constant flame alight, effortlessly, it seemed, for the cooking or the earth-roasting of fish. There were heart of palm and the peculiar fruit of the pandanus, as well as shrimp and octopus and crab; there were delicacies like the small sand shrimp who lived in the muddy soil near my spring, or the seasonal delight of turtle eggs. Each year the females came to lay their eggs on the beach. I could not bring myself to kill them for their meat—they were too rare, too entertaining to me with their slow, thoughtful gazes, but on occasion I took their eggs.

I never tired of my food. Once I had dined with royalty and heads of state, but now I had learned the luxury of simplicity. The imagination was gardener to the most extravagant, exotic herbs and spices; simple juices from flowers and plants needed only the ferment of the mind to become fine wines. I lacked nothing; I lived well.

I led Kuma to my shelter. He watched respectfully, then smiled in surprise when I brought him a driftwood plate heaped with dried fish, taro, and fruit. He reached for the plate and, before touching the food, looked at me gravely and said, "Blessings and peace."

I felt very happy.

As he ate I thought of dreaming, and the unreality of his presence. My burden of solitude had suddenly been lifted, yet I was shy, astonished by his presence, confused by lightness. Would he stay, or leave again in his too-small craft? Would there be room for him on the island, or for me in his canoe?

I asked him the name of this island, almost in fear—should my island be named? Would a name not change it? He laughed and shrugged: "No name, such a wee place!" I laughed too, in relief, and at his curious English—though how beautiful to hear it! I pictured an aging Scottish missionary teaching her flock of small brown boys. He ate, and chuckled too, then said, "But you are near the island of Marakei."

"Marakei?"

"Yes. In the islands of the Kiributs. We are a Buritish colony."

Kiributs. Gilberts. Fred had been right.

Kuma ate everything I gave him. When he had finished he burped and sat back, leaning on his hands. We looked at each other, a shy exchange: Who was the native of this island? Was I still an unexpected guest in his country? I thought of those other unexpected, uninvited guests and asked him about the Japanese.

His English was hesitant at times, but eager. There had been a war, a very big war, all the countries—Europe, the United States,

Japan. The Japanese had occupied many of the islands, not just the Gilberts. Then he demonstrated, his hands speaking again in childlike mime, a bomb falling, just so, a big explosion.

"Japan finished."

"Finished?"

"Too many dead. Go lose war. We go to the Buritish again."

He grew quiet. I thought of the world I had known, fifteen years earlier. All was gone, destroyed or changed forever. A terrible war, like the Great War. Perhaps worse. Yet it had not touched my life beyond the quizzical gaze of a Japanese officer, and the senseless execution of two strangers.

I told him about the two bodies I had found. He frowned and shook his head. "Many bad things. Many things we never know. But it is finished. Now we have peace."

"Kuma, can you take me back with you, to Abaiang?"

He looked at me and I could read his concern, his embarrassment. He quickly shook his head.

"Oh no, it is too far, it is very dangerous."

"You think I care about danger? I cannot stay alone here anymore, you must help me." I reached my hand towards his arm; he withdrew, skittish.

"Oh, I am sorry, it is very far, for me it is very hard journey in one canoe, with two so far is very heavy, I think impossible."

"But Kuma, I can help you, you will be able to sleep and rest—"

Again he shook his head. Again and again, that smooth gesture of refusal; I see it in my sleep. Kuma, like Fred, visits me. Dreams of those heavy moments of my life weigh upon me in sleep, fill me with sadness upon waking, like the sadness on Kuma's face. His sadness was sincere, but his determination—gallantry? superstition? caution?—was greater.

I looked away to the west, to the real place where Abaiang must lie, to the place of people and warmth and love, of children and animals and village feasts, of thatched houses and music and stories. That place could be the beginning of my liberation, of my return to my own kind, but only at great risk to Kuma; he was right, the whitecaps beyond the reef were proof enough of that.

His long, strong fingers played in the sand as he waited for me to speak. I wanted to take those fingers, to plead still, but also to touch, to feel their strength, to know the life of another, to have them curl like a newborn baby's around my own—only it would be me, the newborn.

We sat in silence for some time, and I knew he was, like me, thinking about departure, dreading it, but for a different reason. So I turned to him and said, "Tell me about your island. Tell me about the people there, what you do, how you live . . ."

He smiled, some relief in his face, and for the short time he spent with me on the island, waiting for the wind to abate, for the seas to grow smooth, he told me jolly, confusing stories about Abaiang, which means Land-in-the-Wind.

His voice echoes to me down the years. I hear his stories, though I have forgotten some of the details and added others, in the luxury of retelling. There is one in particular which I tell myself, on those ritual days of remembrance kept not by the calendar but by the urging of the spirit, under a full moon.

In a village on the island of Abemama, which means Land-of-Moonlight, there lived a cousin of Kuma's grandmother. This cousin, Mautake, was a fisherman, a handsome and able young man, whose prowess in his outrigger canoe was legendary throughout the northern islands. He could navigate by the waves, by the currents, by the sun and wind, let alone the stars, and although this ability was not uncommon among the islanders, Mautake also sailed the farthest and caught the most fish in living memory. They called him the Dolphin, and, like his namesake, he had a cheerful and smiling disposition. When he chose a bride, she was the envy of all the young women on the island, for it was believed that extraordinary skills as a fisherman implied equal talent for matrimony.

But the bride he chose was a disappointment to the island's matrons and maidens and their wagging tongues; Tearia was a shy girl, too thin, and it was said she spent too much time listening to the spirits of the dead. They feared her gifts of clairvoyance and failed to understand Mautake's choice. Tearia was, however, unsurpassed in beauty, of an ethereal, fragile kind, as if she were too penetrated by the spirits she spoke to, and not quite of this world.

They proved to be a good match, for Mautake brought cheer and laughter into Tearia's previously serious existence, and she in turn was able to harness some of Mautake's abundant energy and restrain his wilder urges. They lived happily for a time, although they remained childless. Mautake confined his fishing to the lagoon, and on a hand loom Tearia wove beautiful cloth that was the envy of all the women. It was rumored that she wove filaments of the spirits of the dead into her cloth, and that was what gave it such brilliance and lightness.

But these days of happiness were not meant to last, for in both Mautake and Tearia there lay, still, the urgings of their separate destinies, and one day Mautake prepared his canoe to set off beyond the reef once again. He wanted to explore, he said, not just for fish but also to learn about the other islands just beyond the horizon—Kuria, Aranuka. Tearia cried and protested, her face grew long and woeful, but this only hardened Mautake in his resolve. He promised to bring presents from the places he visited, and on a cloudless morning he set out from the lagoon, waving and smiling, for all the world like the dolphins whose company he would soon share.

Tearia returned to her thatched home and her loom to wait. When she tried to weave, the thread tangled and snapped. After several attempts she gave up in restlessness. She could have joined the other village women for conversation, but she felt lonely and uncertain without Mautake. The days of his absence lengthened, and in desperate loneliness one evening she took to communicating with the spirits once again, as the moon rose above the sleeping village.

It was said that the spirits flew low over the rooftops, whistling quietly only to those who knew how to hear. They told of all the events of all the islands—the births, the marriages, the deaths; the arrival of ships, the whereabouts of schools of fish. Tearia had the gift to hear, and thus it was that one night she learned of the death by drowning of her husband Mautake.

Her keening frightened the very ghosts away. The villagers came running and pieced together what had happened from her incoherent cries. They tried to reassure her, to tell her that he would return, that he had not been gone very long, that he was the best navigator in all Abemama, but she would not listen. She obeyed other voices, and gradually the villagers withdrew, leaving her alone with her grief.

The pagan tradition was still very strong at that time, and it was believed that all souls of the dead must transit the northernmost island of Makin-Meang: the edge of the world, the Gate to the Hereafter. At the northernmost tip of the island was the Place of Dread, where the god Nakaa waited in judgment upon the souls of the dead. A good soul, properly buried and mourned, would be allowed passage through the Gate and into the Land of Shades. But a soul who had no proper burial, who had not been mourned according to the prescribed custom, was doomed to suffer strangulation at the hand of Nakaa and writhe forever in his terrible Net.

Tearia knew this was the fate which awaited her husband, for he was *iowawa*, an unburied ghost. He would wander for weeks, waiting and hoping for burial, haunting his village, pleading and hoping, before finally submitting to Nakaa's call.

Tearia did what she could. She chanted and implored the spirits, she sang and danced under the moon, but the village had turned from her in fear, and her mourning alone was not enough to pacify Nakaa. Every night the ghost of Mautake rode through the village, rattling the thatch, upturning water jugs, blowing canoes into the middle of the lagoon, rotting breadfruit on the trees. The villagers were angry with Tearia. They wanted to chase her away; they said Mautake would follow her. Finally she packed some things and left, humble and broken, for a wild windy outcrop of coral where an abandoned fisherman's cottage became her home. The ghost did indeed follow her, and the village was quiet once again.

But there was one person who took pity on Tearia, who watched her lonely exile and felt some of her anguish. This was Teriakai, an older man who was renowned for his bravery yet feared because of his terrible appearance; he had lost a hand to a shark and been badly scarred across the face in the same combat. He was a mild and gentle man, but after the death of his wife in childbirth he had never remarried. He knew no one would have him now, he was old and disfigured, so he passed his time in the lagoon fishing for octopus, and it was said his octopus was the finest in the islands. But if he earned the nickname Octopus, it was not for that reason alone.

Teriakai observed Tearia's sadness and thought she might befriend him. She alone, if anyone, would be able to see into a person's spirit, beyond the body. So he brought her the things she needed in her place of exile and stayed at a respectful distance, waiting, not altogether hopeful, for he had given up that kind of hope long before.

One day Teriakai saw Tearia preparing a small bundle of belongings, as if she was making ready to leave her home. He approached and asked her shyly if she was leaving the island. She smiled and nodded.

"My husband's ghost is restless and tired. He will have no strength left to face the judgment of Nakaa and he fears the great Net. I will go to Makin-Meang, to the Place of Dread, and plant a sprouting coconut in Nakaa's grove. I will accompany my husband's ghost and hope to ease the anger of Nakaa."

Teriakai looked at her in astonishment, seeing her, perhaps, for the first time, in her courage and devotion.

"And how will you get there? It is many days from here!"

She smiled again. "The schooner of the white man will be here at dawn. I will sail to the north with them."

"You should not go alone," said Teriakai. "I can help you."

She shrugged. "Come if you like." Teriakai knew she had no fears and did not need him; he also knew he would suffer far more from her absence than from the rigors of the journey, so together they set out to wait for the schooner.

The people of the village looked on in relief as Tearia and Teriakai boarded the schooner. Tearia would take her last ghosts with her and Teriakai would no longer be there to frighten the young children.

It took them several weeks to reach the northern islands, stopping as they did at each island along the way—Maiana, Tarawa, Abaiang, Marakei—for the white man's business. During that time Tearia and Teriakai stayed huddled at the bow of the boat—the most uncomfortable, dangerous place—as if the constant dousing of waves would wash from them the stain of their difference. They did not leave the ship in port but went below to the hot, airless cabin, where they slept and dreamed. They barely spoke that whole time, almost as if they were not together. The captain was unhappy to have them aboard and was relieved when they reached Butaritari, where he would turn around for the return run to Tarawa. In Butaritari Tearia bought a fine canoe for the last leg to Makin-Meang.

Teriakai spoke at last. "How shall we get there? I have not sailed the open ocean; you have never sailed a canoe," he protested. "We would do better to hire a canoe, with a skipper."

Tearia merely smiled and told him not to worry.

No one watched them leave; no one would ever miss them. They sat in their frail little craft and set out for the Place of Dread with, for all their belongings, a sprouting coconut.

Teriakai watched in wonder as the outrigger skipped along the crests of the waves, guided by some secret force behind Tearia's gentle touch on the tiller.

When they arrived in Makin-Meang, the people of the village there ran in fright from the strange couple. They feared Teriakai's disfigurement; they knew from Tearia's solemn expression and the coconut she carried that she was on a mission of death. Shunned, Tearia and Teriakai began to walk ever northward, to the Place of Dread, along the western shore, as was the custom for strangers to the island. Along that shore, too, walked the ghosts of the dead on their way to meet Nakaa; therefore a living person must never look behind, for fear of seeing the shade of a departed soul.

Did Tearia walk alongside her husband's shade under that burning sun, through the solid wall of wind? Did her husband watch as she planted the seed nut in that desolate grove at the edge of the living world? Was he jealous of the sorry figure, barely more than a shade himself, who followed so faithfully in her footsteps?

They reached the barren sandspit which marked the end, the Place of Dread. Wave and tide met and crashed there, perhaps lifting the departed souls on their way. Tearia stood watching for a long time, seeing beyond the land and the water, following the flight of birds out over the ocean. Teriakai hung back in fear at the edge of Nakaa's grove. He thought of the shark, his own ghost; he thought of death and wondered briefly if he had not, after all, died in the shark's jaws, to wander disfigured in his village until this woman brought him at last to meet Nakaa. But he did not see Nakaa with his terrible Net; he saw no ghosts waiting miserably for judgment. He saw only a small woman on a patch of coral, her long black hair swept out behind her in the wind, her skirts billowing and snapping like a sail. Finally she turned and walked towards him as if to greet him for the first time. She took his hand and led him along the western shore and away from the Place of Dread.

Tearia and Teriakai returned to Butaritari in their canoe and were married some weeks later. They remained on that island, had several children, and found happiness in their new home. People pitied Teriakai for the loss of his hand, but love had eased his features and the terrible scar no longer stared from his face like a threat. Each night Tearia rubbed it with an ointment and the red angry tissue faded away into brown, into a smile loved by all, but by small children in particular.

Tearia took up her weaving again, but she complained that the thread was not of the quality to be found on Abemama.

Her children often asked to hear stories of the spirits, but she had to repeat the old ones until they grew bored with them, for the air above their thatched roof echoed no other sound than the rustling of palm trees in the wind.

*

For me there is no Place of Dread, no appeasement of the god memory. Shades whistle over my shelter in the night, in the early hours; I cannot chase them, for they are my only company.

Iowawa. Unhappy, restless spirit, condemned to wandering in my memory.

I wish I could tell all of Kuma's stories as he told them, with his eyes crinkling in laughter at remembrance, his giggles spilling over his cheeks and down his chin at the joy of their telling. And Kuma—Kuma himself is another story, one with no ending. I do not know what happened out there beyond the edge of blue, beyond the edge of my world. He set out on the third day, when the storm clouds were gone and the winds once again blew favorably from the northeast. I filled his canoe with food; he filled me with a promise to deliver a letter for me to the head of the village. "A big boat will come for you, with real engine," he said. "A Yankee engine, yes, good strong engine!"

He slipped into his fragile craft, lighter than air, than wind, than life, and said, "*Ko na mauri*—it means, blessings and peace are ours."

"Blessings and peace," I echoed, and helped to push him away from the land.

I watched until he was no more, his smallness and vulnerability lost into the space beyond. There were whitecaps that day; he was one of them.

As I waited, I repeated Kuma's stories to myself, trying to retain the sound of his voice, the rhythm of his laughter. I lay awake at night and saw him as he had been, sleeping at the foot of the shelter where Fred had once slept. I saw him brown and young and alive, and marveled at his existence. He was child-tender as he slept. I had wanted so much to touch him.

I waited and dreamed of Kuma and the return of a boat full of strong islanders and a Yankee engine; I waited for its music in the distance. I thought, foolishly, indulgently, of my husband and mother and sister and the larger world beyond Abaiang, and the welcome I would find there.

I waited and did not see the parched blueness of the sky. The endless days of sunshine were there to celebrate my coming deliverance. I did not see that the frangipani failed to bloom, that the island was growing dry with waiting, that the fish emptied from the lagoon. The sharks came in abundance in their hunger and then I knew that I too was hungry. But I did not care, I had Kuma's stories of village feasts to feed me. The drought grew worse—the spring reduced to a mere trickle—and I felt my body drying with the island.

I waited for a very long time. How long had Kuma been gone? My calendar told me it was already five months. Hope and stories had sustained me all that time, but on the day I found that the spring had dried up, I understood he would not return. I saw again the small craft pulling gracefully into the distance, into a land of forgetfulness, perhaps into death itself, into the land of Nakaa. There had been storms a few days after his departure—the last terrible winds before the drought. I had tried to put the storms out of my mind in my need to believe, but at the time I had lain in my shelter and prayed, in my way, for Kuma's safety.

But it was for myself that I had prayed, really; I had prayed to leave the island and return to my own kind, to my former life, to ease and comfort and the company of presidents. I had prayed for that Yankee engine, not for that simple handmade canoe.

I believe I nearly died then. Of grief, of hunger. There was nothing left to eat, and very little water, only what I had saved in two jugs. I had no strength to break open the coconuts. The few fish left in the lagoon were claimed by the sharks. Small crabs crawled to me, full of pity. I lay in the shelter and waited.

One morning I awoke and left the shelter and walked, hunger-feeble, to the spot where I had first seen Kuma's footprints. I sat in the sand and looked at the clouds stacked on the horizon, baroque, whorled, empty. I smoothed the sand by the place where the footprints had been, over and over, until it lay flat and pure in that small space like a table made bare for a meal. I lay there and slept until the sun was too hot and then I returned to my shelter.

*

By late afternoon the air was thick, the light darkening, storm-rich. I went to the beach. The clouds were now black, tumbling with menace. Distant thunder followed streaks of lightning. White horses were ridden with spray beyond the reef; the palm branches twisted in apprehension.

I stood on the beach by Kuma's vanished footprints and remembered it all—how the island had saved Fred and me and looked after us, fed us, given us that first great gift. How it had saved me from the Japanese and brought me a wealth of food and flowers. How it had taken pity on me and brought me Kuma, and his stories with which to embroider my loneliness. I was a native of this island.

The sky opened at last, bursting with relief, abundant with sorrow and repentance. The rains returned and the flowers soon bloomed; the island grew green and rich and welcomed me. I too had returned.

I would like to know them, the couple on the sailboat. I would like to go to them and say, *Ko na mauri*. But the future hurt of their departure is contained in their presence.

I could leave with them, after all; am I not free?

While they were on my island, I went to their boat. They need water. I filled my water jugs and ferried what I could to them, borrowing their small rubber boat. I marveled at the movement—rowing—disused for so many years, since my own raft . . .

I poured the water into a bronze fitting marked "water"—what a clever, organized world on such a small boat! I explored the cabin—so quickly, for fear they would return—I even spoke on the radio, calling into the airwaves, my voice trembling, forty-two years too late. I saw the neat little galley with its row of colorful mugs; the double berth, like the bed of a maharaja to me; the gleaming white toilet! I saw their books: many long-forgotten classics, many unfamiliar titles in small, flimsy editions. I opened a drawer and it was full of clothing, made of fabrics which seemed strange to my inexperienced fingers.

On the wooden paneling hung photographs, in bright, clear colors, and I was able to pause and study their faces, looking at me from the site of a ruined castle. They were so young; I could see an arrogant innocence in their faces, an ignorance of the peril and fragility of their journey.

Above the toilet there was a mirror. I did not look. The lagoon suffices; I was afraid I would see the marks, too deep, too permanent, of my own journey.

*L*ucy has to overcome her fear of the island. Robin has shown her that logically, rationally, there is nothing to fear. The hours she spends on the boat expand with resentment and impatience; the constant clank of tools reminds her that she is stranded and that her release depends on Robin. Her ignorance and helplessness cause her to mutter and fume. She gets in his way; they swear at each other.

She remembers the serenity of the moment in the small cove on the eastern shore and finally, one afternoon, with her face set in mock determination, she sets off in the dinghy with the hope of recapturing that lost moment.

The lagoon is a lake of liquid jewel; shifting colors shot with sunlight cause her to catch her breath as she rows, to pause in her strokes, letting clarity drip from her oars as the light folds around her.

On the island there are bushes of flowers, deep crimson. She pauses as she walks; she does not remember flowers. Have they just bloomed? What strange seasons do they keep? She picks one and puts it in her hair. It makes her feel young, beautiful. In this moment, where no one can see her, she borrows from the island's youth and purity, from its constant regeneration.

She sits on the beach, not far from where she saw the footprint. She has decided that islanders must, on occasion, visit the island for some sort of fishing. That is all; they would not harm her.

But she thinks of Robin and knows that harm of a kind lies that way, in their failure to love. Because they are together, they take for granted the idea of their love—is it only an idea, an assumption no longer based on reality?

What dreamers they are. They dream of earthly paradises; they have dreamed of eternal love. They know that eternal love is an idea for romance novels and religious ceremonies, not something which can be sustained throughout a lifetime. And yet, still they pretend—from fear of solitude? Out of loyalty to the origins of their love? Or can they hope for more, for a comfortable future of warm companionship?

Lucy looks inward now. The island withdraws, a backdrop to her memories. Her first meeting with Robin was not romantic. A glance of curiosity, a nod, exchanged at the first staff meeting she attended when newly employed at the school. The meeting within the meeting, they had joked, much later, in the time when they savored every small irony or coincidence which could enhance their sense of wonder.

She has loved deeper, harder, truer, before Robin. More passionately, some would say, but she dislikes the word. Passion, to be successful, must self-destruct, allowing no deterioration into the realm of the ordinary—no rising together to go to work, no dirty socks, no leftovers in front of the television. Lucy accepts the loss of passion.

She lies back upon the sand. Faces appear, indistinct, blurred by years. Each belongs to a different period of her life and of her apprenticeship of men and love. She holds them, some with sadness, others with bemusement; she feels more regret for the passing of time than for the face in the memory.

The first time. A tiny room in an attic; the dusty light of late afternoon sprawled across the carpet. He knocked and came in quietly, for she had been napping. Like her, he was a student; they shared notes and reference books and coffee breaks, always looking at each other with eyes that were too bright for mere intellectual exchange, always apologizing for the accidental touching that betrayed their confusion. He sat on her bed as if he had decided— if she was willing, he would take her to that place she had only read and heard, and perhaps dreamed, about. She was afraid, but willing; in exchange for her innocence he gave her the insatiability of shared exploration. They were happy; they studied, made love, ate hasty meals at one o'clock in the morning, made love again. Drove to the ocean during snowstorms; camped their way through the north of Norway. Then one day it seemed there was nothing left to explore. They had reached an empty space where their gestures and laughter rang hollow. They drifted apart, and Lucy wondered if she had really loved.

Some years later, a sunlit hotel room in a hot western city; traffic noises punctuated hurried lovemaking. He was a married man, they had so little time together. Neither wore a watch, they could not bear to be reminded of life's constraints. So they stole the time from passers-by, peering at bare suntanned wrists, just as they stole the time from his wife and children. There was never enough of it; they could never get enough of each other. One day he began to wear his watch again, and Lucy knew it was over. The sun-filled hours remained forever suspended out of time in her memory; she often wondered if her life since then had not been a fruitless search for another sunlit hotel room. She knew by then that she may have already experienced the most joyful, intense moments of her life.

Then she became rational, reasonable, somewhat cynical; much time was spent in cafés and libraries and a new man entered her life through her mind. He shared her convictions about art; he shared long, impassioned late-night discussions about everything that mattered to her, from Simone de Beauvoir to Vietnam. Finally he shared her bed, and their disappointment was astonished and mutual. They parted friends, but the fire had gone out of their discussions, leaving something cold and empty they were both afraid of.

It is more than the passing of time that Lucy regrets; it is the loss of a certain privileged pact with life, of being allowed to place her hand upon its very pulse to feel its mysterious strength and energy.

With Robin she feels she has lost that privilege. It has been all plans ("our future") and worries ("the end of the month"), lightened occasionally by entertainment ("I've got two tickets . . ."). And sex. Familiar, well-oiled, refined, and too, too predictable.

She looks away into the indifferent distance, not focusing but staring into the space within herself. She hates to think in this way about Robin; she cares very deeply about him. She cares about their future; after all, they have a history together, tightly bound with both friendship and suffering—the initial uncertainties, then later disappointments, minor jealousies, illnesses. They have their inside jokes, their bearable bad habits and idiosyncrasies, their hatred of loneliness. They present a well-matched, united front to the world. People say they have the real thing.

To Lucy there is a question of meaning, of vocabulary. Love. In English, a word often abused and misapplied, too vague, and frayed with overuse. Other languages seem to offer more nuance—Greek has *erota* and *agape*, Italian *innamoramento* and *amore*; French, on the other hand, does worse with *aimer* for to like or to love and must rely on modifiers (*un peu, beaucoup, passionnément*). Russian *sounds* right, with *lyoubov'*, all mystery and softness and complication, but is that not merely its exotic, unfamiliar resonance? Why not have a dozen words for love—as the Eskimos do for snow? Wherever you look, she concludes, language is both inadequate and inaccurate, and, in this case, forces the collective imagination to strive for something unreal, virtually unattainable. Eternal love.

She loves Robin, but she does not know what that means anymore.

Lucy curls up against the sand and thinks of the married man. While he and Lucy were living this ecstatic, exalted *thing*, as they used to call it, for lack, once again, of an appropriate word, running away together on "business weekends" or "conventions," the rest of the time he and his wife were living this other *thing* (with two children, on top of it), this Robin-and-Lucy quotidian existence, what-do-you-want-for-supper-have-you-seen-my-keys. At the time, Lucy became aware that this seemed to be the way of many relationships, let alone marriage; she had sworn she would never marry, or at any rate never allow children to enter the relationship with their demands for attention, their extreme possessiveness. Her lover had laughed at her. You'll see, you all want it, the wedding ring, the babies, in the end. And he had been right, but only partially. She had wanted, and got, the marriage, but she still did not want the children.

Everyone told her she was wrong, but she could not see it any other way, not yet.

Her lover was still married to the same woman; his children were grown. He and his wife had also set off on a sailboat, somewhere.

Dreaming. Escaping. Trying to keep love eternal, feeding it with coconut palms and blue lagoons.

She hates her cynicism, she hates the whole clichéd, worn-out world. The lack of words, the loss of meaning.

Stop, Lucy, she tells herself, you are alone on this island. Robin is not here. You are quite alone, you are no longer defined by being part of a couple, loving or otherwise; you must be yourself. Forgive him, it is not his fault, it is yours for dragging him into every corner of your being until you can no longer find yourself without him.

Look around. Look at this place—remember what you felt the other day, before you were frightened away from here and into his protective arms.

The wind has risen and caresses her as her first lover once did. Gentle, exploring. She lies, her eyes closed, and feels. And listens. A music, like singing—eerie, haunting. It is singing. She should be frightened, but she isn't. A sweet, high note. She inhales the soft baby-powder scent of the frangipani.

The island sings to her, like a lover.

*

She returns to the boat, her arms laden with frangipani and hibiscus. Robin looks at her, astonished, an eyebrow raised in irony, then returns to the engine room. Lucy, disappointed because he has said nothing, thrusts the flowers into a vase, casually, almost spitefully. Flowers are not enough to rouse him from his grease-coated apathy.

When she goes into the main cabin to start supper, the flowers hang sadly, wilted, their brilliance lost. Lucy is dismayed; she had not thought they would fade so quickly.

She will take Robin with her tomorrow, to gather more.

But in the early morning, when they walk together on the island, there are no flowers in their path. Robin teases her and uses for the first time the word to describe the mystery: "It's the footprint *ghost* who's picked all the flowers." He doesn't care, his thoughts are on the engine. But Lucy feels tricked and foolish; he has mocked her, and she doubts her own sanity.

That evening it is his turn to feel foolish. He begins by upending cushions, then opening lockers and pulling their contents into the light. Finally he turns to her and asks if she has seen the paperback he was reading.

"You left it in the magazine rack by the starboard bunk."

"That's what I thought, but it's not there."

"Look in the V-berth."

"I haven't had it in there. You always move my things out during the day. I can't find anything now."

"Well, I'm sorry. I don't know."

Lucy returns to her own book, puzzled, but indifferent. He's always losing things.

Robin does not see it that way. There are things which are important—tools, engine parts, exam papers to be marked—which he never misplaces. He is careful and organized with those things. But the rest, the ordinary clutter of a shared life—coffee cups, keys, paperbacks—he considers unimportant and, unconsciously, he confers responsibility for them onto Lucy.

Restless at the prospect of an evening without entertainment, he broods. He wonders if his scientific background has made him less able to analyze the subtleties of their marriage than Lucy. He lacks the words, the nuances; he tends to polarize, black and white. You won't have my child, therefore you don't love me enough; if you really loved me, you would have more faith in me. Sometimes he becomes aware of this shortcoming, with a flash of intuition, and spends several hours huddled over a restaurant table with Lucy in deep complicity, in winged communication. But for the most part, the obstructions of daily life blur his vision and leave him confused, stubborn and impatient.

His brief affair gave him a glimpse of another life, another self. Everything was clear, intense, sharp. There was no mess; there were no silences, no dark looks. Lovemaking, too, seemed to follow its own logic, perfectly timed, effortless, full of élan. Robin had not known what to do about the situation, however—he felt so amazingly good with this young woman, but he also knew he had an investment of time with Lucy, and that on a template of responsible behavior in his imagination he saw her, and not the other woman, as the mother of his children. And he could not understand—science, of course, offered no explanation—why his affair suddenly ended, without a word. He later heard that she had moved in with a young man she'd once referred to as her "old" boyfriend; for once the irony of language was not lost on Robin. Who was old, now?

Now he sees the repair of the engine as more than a merely mechanical necessity: it has taken on symbolic importance. Yet it eludes him, frustrates him in ways that are beyond comprehension, trying his patience and perseverance yet denying him the option of giving up. He struggles with the huge manual, leaving black thumbprints like bear tracks across its pages as he frowns at diagrams and glibly incomplete instructions. To make things worse, Lucy does not really understand how much he hates engine work now; she must think he actually enjoys it (her forced, bright interest), whereas he expects some other treatment—sympathy, even compassion—accompanied by cups of coffee and cuddles, as if the engine room were a sick bay.

When Lucy does not find his book he goes to bed but lies awake for a long time, feigning sleep. At dawn he cannot face starting another day in the cramped hole they call the engine "room"; he rises while Lucy sleeps and goes up on deck.

They are anchored several hundred feet from the beach—an easy swim, were it not for the sharks. Robin stands on deck for several minutes, watching, looking: the lagoon is pristine, undisturbed. He dives into its thick transparency and heads for shore with regular, unhurried strokes. He has heard that sharks attack only fear. That is logical, he thinks as he swims: in Nature's plan, the weaker members of each species know their weakness from bitter experience, and therefore cannot control their fear. Thus they signal to the stronger, despite themselves, and bring on their own demise, in compliance with Nature's grand scheme.

As a scientist, Robin must remain skeptical, particularly of his own theory, but he has arrived safely on shore and stands, without fear, at the edge of the island.

$\mathcal{N}$ow the man Robin has come alone. He stands on the beach and stretches. He is a golden color, his hair and beard are pale, sun-whitened. He stands, a conquering Viking with his stretching and looking. He has swum from the boat; he is naked.

Of course he cannot know I am here, would not expect, on a desert island, to show modesty. Though he always comes clothed with his wife. And she comes clothed, alone.

I have never been able to bring myself to leave off my clothes. There is my own modesty towards myself; also a fear of the sun and of insects. The clothes are terribly worn and faded, but still serve. When there is no rain I wash them in the lagoon, leaving the wind to whip what salt it can from the cloth.

Sometimes when I swim in the lagoon, I remove them; this is my bath. And I come out and drip away age. I look and my body is as young and firm as it was when I arrived here. I do not know if that is what others would see; that is what I see.

The man begins to run and I am quite moved by his nakedness. There is something of the wild in him after all, with that long hair and all-brown body—no swimsuit mark of civilization. He is motion and freedom, quite at home here. He runs along the beach, for the sake of running—the measured stride, the smooth working of his muscles.

I watch until he reaches the spit at the south end of the island. He will turn now, and come back; he must not find me here.

In my shelter there is a new treasure, a novel. *The French Lieutenant's Woman.* I have taken it from them—they might miss it, of course, but I think that if they could ever know the pleasure it will give me they would not mind. I have been torn between honesty and selfishness; must I read it quickly and put it back, or dare I keep it to read over and over, for the pleasure?

As it happens, I cannot read quickly. I am not used to letters on a page anymore. My eyes tire and long-forgotten words demand time. I read aloud, quietly; words and voice struggle together against neglect. Yet I can savor the words and the pictures they convey; I read certain passages over and over. It is very beautiful. But the story takes second place to the words at present. I am like a child, learning to read, learning the world I have forgotten.

I have been reading in the shade of my shelter; I hear the drumming of the man's footfall, quite close now. They have never found me — mere accident, or am I grown quite invisible?

I hear a pause, then steps falling away again in the direction of the lagoon. I leave the book and follow. The words will wait.

He starts to walk into the lagoon but then runs out again, quickly. A fin circles close to shore; I recognize a big, old shark with a characteristic mark on his fin. He is a bully, I have seen him chase every form of wildlife from the lagoon. I call him Kaiser Bill; I wait, when he is there.

The man Robin waits too, no ease in his waiting. He shouts, a clear, fine sound on the morning: "Lucy!" He waits, but there is no response.

He is impatient. With the ways of the city he strides, turns, looks down, up, over, kicks the sand, sits, stands again. The shark glides, as smooth as the man is nervous. Back and forth, a sentry.

Then another fin approaches; this is unusual. Although the sharks sometimes come in groups, they usually avoid this old bully.

To and fro they glide, stubbornly, between the shore and the sailboat. The man calls again, louder, an edge to his voice.

And now, a third shark.

Should I warn him? The sharks can smell his fear.

We wait as the heat rises. Lucy does not answer the calls; Kaiser Bill and his companions do not tire of their game. I sit and wonder if I can help without revealing myself. He sits in a spot of shade, back from the beach; I hide several hundred feet away. Perhaps I would frighten him more than the sharks do.

Then Lucy is there, on the deck, shouting, concern in her voice. He leaps up and calls back to her.

"I can't get back, there are three sharks here now. Can you get the outboard onto the dinghy and make a dash for it?"

"Oh God." She wipes her hair from her forehead. "Let's wait. Let's hope they'll leave."

I observe their city-trained measure of time, as she calls out intervals, as he moves in restlessness. That time was once mine: schedules, appointments, engagements, lectures, requirements and restrictions of a life of importance and success. Every clock-driven minute was invoiced, accountable.

The island has taught me another time. At first it was hard. Fred and I used the almanac as our calendar, folding back the pages with the passing days; then 1937 was no more. We started the almanac again but soon gave up—we would wear out the pages. So it became knife-cuts on a piece of wood. Each day was crossed off, like a red line through a prisoner's sentence.

We also made a sundial, adjusting the set of the dial by Fred's watch, until it was quite accurate. In that way we had a second timepiece. We took great interest in the accuracy of the sundial—it was a game. The first time Fred forgot to wind his watch we realized we would no longer have an accurate reading, only an approximation of the time we had once been governed by to live, to navigate. It was a first relinquishment of the hold the past had on us.

After Fred was gone I would look at the sundial and the time it displayed had become meaningless. How could we have been so controlled, so governed by a mere shadow on a wooden disk full of notches?

But time was so precious then, too.

The dial broke during a storm. It lies somewhere in a pile of undergrowth and island refuse.

I stopped notching the days on the calendar after Kuma did not return. I had waited for five months believing he would come back for me; five months stretched into perpetuity which live still, in memory and in loss.

Now I mark only the months, with the passage of the moon, and sometimes I forget even that. Time has no meaning; there are no longer any boundaries. Only solitude; only seasons, cycles. That is not time, it is the natural breathing of the earth.

He shouts at her, his impatience is too great. I can sense her trembling—minute waves across the lagoon—as she lifts the small engine from the deck into the dinghy, as she clings for last safety to the edge of the sailboat. Then she is sitting in the boat, screwing the engine onto its bracket, watching nervously for the sharks.

The animals do not pause in their patrol of the beach. She will have to time her arrival to reach her husband when they are as far away as they will go, and trust to their seemingly stupid predictability to seize her chance; they may not oblige. She knows this.

She fires the engine and waits to see if the sharks react. One of them veers away from the old one and heads out towards the pass; the other two persist. She pauses, gauging their speed against hers, then sets off with a burst of the throttle as she shifts into gear.

The sharks are headed away from her, on their southbound leg. She aims for Robin, he runs knee-deep into the lagoon. Old Kaiser Bill is turning, leaving the smaller shark behind—do I merely imagine that he is going faster? Lucy slows down, Robin runs, splashes, flops belly-first into the dinghy; she turns about and speeds away, nearly spilling her husband into the lagoon. The shark reaches them, follows a few yards behind, briefly, for sport; then skulks away towards the pass.

Robin's voice is full of relief and praise; Lucy does not speak. She knows that a mere rubber boat is not protection against a shark. She has learned something of the greed of time, as of sharks.

It is evening now.

They will be leaving soon, I think. I have heard the engine of the sailboat humming as never before. I have heard their cries of jubilation as it started, and ran, and did not cough or splutter.

I must decide.

There is the island. There are my forty-two years here. If indeed they are forty-two. More than half my life spent on this island, but years no longer count, their significance no greater than a turning tide, a waning moon. I have learned other measures.

But for all this, I had to redefine my world, and my place in it.

Fred was gone. For months all space was filled with hopelessness. But even the very lack of hope had held a last link with humanity—both mourning and a reaching out for consolation. I had been mourner and consoler, worshiper and worshiped, talker and listener. I was my own society—but could I speak of society? Could I even speak of existence? I knew I existed—heat and hunger and pain confirmed that I did—but what of my soul, unanswered, unheard?

I thought about religion. I thought it might not matter, being abandoned and forgotten here, if this was God's chosen place for me on earth, because I would be able to talk to him and a new-born faith would confirm to me the wisdom of my solitude. I lay on the beach and watched the stars rise to wheel their way across the darkness; I spoke, I prayed, I listened. I thrust myself into the depths of the night sky, but for all the brightness of the stars there was only an echoing wilderness, a reverberating emptiness. A tinkling rattle of stars. God was not ready with his answer.

That left only me, and the island.

*

I thought I had a choice, not much of one, but a choice never-theless. I could surrender to my circumstances, to the idea of a savage, brutal wilderness; I could be a living sacrifice. I would ex-ist as a mere animal, eating, sleeping, evacuating, surviving. I could forget my so-called humanity—my education, language, manners, humor, emotions. This would be a living death of a kind: mindless, joyless, but perhaps painless. There might be some salvation, from somewhere, someday.

Or I could pretend to maintain society. Maintain the illusion of humanity. Read my old navigation tables yet again, speak to myself, eat with a spoon, laugh at the sport of the birds and fish, wear my clothes and keep them clean, wonder at the beauty of clouds, of a summer thunderstorm. I would be the little monarch of an unpeopled kingdom; I would be my own subject.

Of course I chose the latter route. I never stopped hoping that if I kept my humanity, if I kept up a pretense of waiting for rescue but learned all the while to love the island for its simple beauties, I might eventually be rewarded by a return to civilization.

My rewards have not been what I expected. Perhaps they have been greater; the truth lies somewhere between the two choices I envisioned so many years ago.

I sometimes wonder if the Japanese did not kill me, after all. My life here has been in the nature of a long dream, hazed like the smoke from the funeral pyre. Did I not die then, too?

There have been the small, unexplained miracles, vivid dreams from which I cannot wake. The abundance of fruit and flowers where before there had been none. Lightning storms of intense beauty, illuminating the world—at times I can see all the islands spread like stars across the vastness of the Pacific.

And one night, when the air was very still and so hot that move-ment became painful, I lay and remembered snow. I thought for many hours of all the snowy vistas I had seen, all the childhood snowstorms. I fell asleep picturing the slowly falling flakes. When I awoke at dawn and crept from my shelter, a fine cloth of white lay upon the island, and the last tiny flakes melted away in the first rays of the sun.

Such things do not happen in that other world, beyond the horizon: only here, on this island.

But there were times when I thought I could not accept Nature's heavy burden. I would lie awake at night and listen to the percussion of insects while I stared at the sorrowful gibbous moon. The absurdity of my presence here—on that palm-woven mat, under that palm-woven awning, when less than a hundred miles away there were people dancing and laughing—called upon an implacable warder to stand over my pallet as I writhed and called out for deliverance.

The island taught me, after Kuma disappeared, the futility of wishing to be elsewhere. Of course I wanted to be rescued, to be restored to my family and loved ones, but that was a life in the past, or in the future. Now I was on the island, and to value my life I had to learn to love the present.

(In all my mad quest for records in aviation—the most ironic of all, the "solo" achievements—and in all my mad dashing around the planet, did I ever know the present? Was I not always too busy trying to break into some other dimension—a place in the future sure to guarantee my immortality, because of my feats in the past? My bitter, strange success; my unexpected reward.)

Now, a frigate bird, circling, curious about the sailboat in the lagoon; he will perch upon the mast and have a rest . . .

Now, the sun so low on the horizon, poised on an emerald ocean-edge of luminescence. It has been thus for tens of thousands of days, hardly varying, but now and always the scene is refulgent with beauty in its regular passage . . .

Now, Lucy and Robin in their cockpit watching that same sunset. Will it be their last on the island? Do they know it, and does that knowledge make the sunset more intense, touched with the gentle melancholy of departure, the anticipation of nostalgia? Are they already in the future?

If I imagine, now, leaving the island, the sky darkens, the trees grow wild, wind-thrashed.

The island shows me my own reflection in the still waters of the lagoon.

The island has made a terrible pact with me over the years.

The island wants me to stay, and has offered me something unnatural—like snow at the equator—in exchange for my future.

$\mathcal{S}$he can hardly bear to speak to him. She wants to punish him with her silence; it is the only way of creating distance and space between them. She knows she should feel something different—perhaps some sort of pride, or compassion, for having rescued him from the sharks, but as she tries, unsuccessfully, to sleep through the torpor of mid-afternoon, she is revisited by his impatience and by the taunting insolence of Nature in the form of the shark. Instead of pride she feels humiliation, a powerless rage which she can neither explain nor control.

Nerves, perhaps. Nature at work within her. She puts her hand on her belly, wishing for the reassuring ache which comes each month to remind her of her freedom. But she has been neglectful of science, of rigor: on the awful night of their arrival at the island, and then again on the night after she saw the footprint, she forgot to take her pill, remembering it only the following evening. Would science forgive? How late was too late? She tries not to think about it, not to care, weighing odds in her favor. But what if it does not come this month; what if, because of everything which has happened . . .

She refuses to think about it. Instead she watches the pair of dark-gray fins, back and forth, up and down, patrolling her imagination.

He turns the key. A few clicks, then a successful cough and the engine finds its voice, midway between hum and roar, lubricated and content. He lets out a war whoop, and stands back to listen to her chug. Lucy appears behind him, her hair a tangle across her forehead.

"This is it!" he shouts. "We can leave tomorrow at the first slack tide!"

She smiles, but evades his outstretched arm, dancing gracefully aside on her way to the galley.

He looks at her, puzzled; she has not stopped smiling.

"Lu?"

She shrugs and turns her back to him, to look for the coffee.

Perhaps it's just a game, he thinks with a sigh; she'll tire of it when she thinks she's punished me enough.

She holds the hot mug in her palms and looks around her. The island turns and stretches in the late-afternoon sun, coating itself in the golden light, preparing for darkness. She will be glad to leave. The desolation seems to bring out the worst in her. One man's society is not enough, she realizes. They cannot be all things to each other.

He joins her and sits silently, swirling a dark liquid in a small glass. Then he breaks the calm by saying something trivial — nice evening, or, glad to be out of here soon — something trivial and forced and meaningful only for its attempt to break through to her. She says nothing, then lets out a deep, exasperated, uncontrollable sigh. She looks away, then at him, and with great surprise and relief he sees that there are tears in her eyes. She always tries, so hard, so hard, to keep it in, to be strong, to keep from breaking. He reaches for her; he marvels, not for the first time, at how easy — and how difficult — it can be to close the gap. They move together and sit closely, watching the sun. He dries her tears. They do not speak. For now, there is no need.

In the early morning they go ashore, one last time. They are waiting for slack water, when the pass will be calmer.

The island lies hushed with stillness. A few birds call out at their passage, astonished by morning visitors. They tread softly, respectfully, as if in a graveyard. Robin remarks on this; Lucy laughs softly and says, "Graveyard, no. But spirits, perhaps."

When they reach the eastern beach, Lucy looks out at the horizon, then shouts excitedly. "Robin! Look, way out there, a ship!"

He squints but does not see the ship at first; she aims his gaze down her arm. "There. See it? It's a ship, no?"

The structure on the bridge, a slight interruption in the endless blue line, several miles away. He nods.

"Shall we go back and call it on the radio? Come on, let's!" she says.

"Oh, Lu, can't we leave it now? We'll be gone from here in a few hours, I'd rather enjoy the island while we can—"

"Enjoy!? Oh, come on, we need to know where we are—"

"You go back. We can't leave yet anyway, I'll stay here for a bit."

Incredulous, she looks at him, then sets off at a run towards the dinghy.

Robin watches her brown body disappear among the trees. Once again, he sighs, I have sinned. She'll be thinking I am too careless, irresponsible. I'm the skipper, I should be concerned, I should want to know where I am. Instead I stay here on this godforsaken atoll, wandering around looking at coconuts and seashells, like some sightseeing two-week tourist . . .

But not for much longer. The prospect of departure makes him nervous—it always does—but glad, too. Lucy will be better, happy to be moving again, to a place where they will be among people again. The tension between them is normal, really, he thinks; they have been under a lot of strain, stranded here, with so little relief from each other or from the demands of the boat; the island itself hardly welcoming—footprints, disappearing flowers, honestly . . .

He can just make out the ship on the horizon, northbound. To the Marshalls, or Hawaii? There is no major shipping route near here, but perhaps it has called at one of the islands farther south.

Tea and spices, he muses. Robin knows he has a romantic side, rooted in regret. Why was he not born fifty or a hundred years earlier, when there were still frontiers for everyone, when he could have been an adventurer, when such a calling was still practical, often lucrative? He had ancestors who had emigrated to Kenya, others to Patagonia. They had done well out there, as planters, ranchers. There was also the story of an American great-grandfather who had been captain of a whaling ship out of Massachusetts.

But now choices like those had gone the way of most colonies—virtually nonexistent, tainted with the legacy of exploitation. Nowadays, if you were a pragmatist, you went into business or finance; if you were a pragmatist looking for the last frontiers, you went into science. Robin had no sympathy for bankers and financiers; he thought of them as too rapacious, self-serving. So that left science. But Robin had not been brilliant, and the few job offers made to him after he got his degree had been ethically questionable. So he had gone into teaching. And had disguised his romantic notions as a hobby, until now, when *Stowaway* would, at last, evoke something of the old seafaring life as she bent to the trades.

He is ready to leave now, to be back in those trades, Tarawa-bound; from there, perhaps, the Solomons, then Australia, where they might spend some time, perhaps start a family, thinks Robin, at last . . .

"Robin! Robin!" She is calling him, excited; he turns to get her news of the ship, then sees her face. "What's wrong, Lucy?"

"The dinghy's gone. *Gone!*"

"What? Has it drifted into the lagoon, didn't we pull it far enough onto the sand?"

"I don't know; come quickly, please!"

Breathless, she tells him how she came down upon the beach to find the empty space where they always left the dinghy, how she had looked in panic out towards the reef—had the wind carried it far out, to the sharks' domain and beyond, irretrievable? She could not see it. She did not wait to look further, but turned and ran back to Robin. "It's absurd," she concludes; "it's like being back in the city—the time the bike got stolen, or the car stereo—but who? No, it has to be the wind."

They have reached the lagoon; *Stowaway* sits at anchor, poster-pretty, unreal. In the foreground, beached on the sand like a small sea mammal, lies their gray inflatable dinghy.

Robin looks at her, gently places his palm on her forehead as she mutters and babbles incomprehensible explanations. He silences her, then says softly, "You're going mad here, you're imagining things. You've had too much sun."

"No, I promise you—"

"Promise me what?"

She begins to giggle, and her giggles turn to laughter as Robin lifts her up and carries her to the water's edge. When they are in three feet of water he drops her, gently, and slips as he does, falling upon her and then away, his laughter joining hers.

How good to laugh. How good to forget the strain between them. They laugh and hug and look for a moment at each other in stunned delight; then Lucy remembers the ship.

"Calling unidentified vessel to northeast of . . . unidentified island. Do you read me?"

The radio is quiet. Lucy waits. The ship's radio officer will have to pick up the transmitter, perhaps wait for her to repeat her own call, which she does, eager for a voice to come booming, welcome, over the air.

"This is the sailing vessel *Stowaway*. Do you copy? Come in, please."

The radio is silent.

Robin watches sadly. He knows that, even though they are ready to leave and a series of sun sights will give them their position by nightfall, Lucy still needs to know from someone, out there, where they are; and she needs to tell that same someone that she is here.

"Wait a minute," she says to Robin, something new in her voice.

"What?"

"The radio was *on*. I'm sure it was, but I didn't switch it on. Yes, I'm sure; I just grabbed the receiver, I didn't switch it on."

"Well, you left it on from last time, whenever that was—"

"No, no, I'm sure I switched it off then. The last time I called was ages ago, two, three days. I've been switching it off ever since you began to worry about depleting the ship's batteries. We would have noticed. But it was *on* just now."

"Perhaps I switched it on and forgot," says Robin, helpful. "Just checking, you know."

She smiles, relieved.

But Robin knows he has not touched the radio.

They set about their separate tasks to prepare the boat for departure. Lucy removes the awning and sail covers from the deck, stows them, then goes below to begin stowing and lashing in the galley and cabin. Robin inspects the fuel filters and then, more out of curiosity than necessity, shines his flashlight into the water-tank locker—they have been very careful with their water consumption. Lucy watches from the galley, a look of concern on her face.

"Have we got enough left to get to Tarawa?"

He says nothing for a moment, then switches off the flashlight and looks at her. "I think we have enough to get to Australia."

"Stop kidding."

"Come and have a look. There's more than when we last checked. The tanks are nearly full."

"Go on. Salt water must be getting in, we must have a leak somewhere, oh God—"

"Don't panic, Lu. If it was salty, you'd taste it."

They look at each other across the soft gloom of the cabin, separately wondering what strange magic has come to inhabit their small world.

*

The engine purrs, and Lucy, standing at the wheel, eases the boat forward while Robin raises the anchor. She is excited; in less than twenty-four hours they will be at Tarawa, among people again. There will be the welcome from the local population; there will be the camaraderie of the boating community—other boats with tales to tell, and time to listen.

She glances back at the beach, at the coconut palms nodding in the morning breeze. She has known some happiness there, a privileged moment of revelation, a glimpse into an unexplored part of herself, into something beyond herself. But she is also suspicious of such moments; they do not last, and one never knows where and when they might recur, like islands of an uncharted archipelago.

Robin raises his hand with the gesture to stop forward motion; she hears the cranking of the windlass; their tie to the island is being broken. He shouts to her to put the engine in gear again, and they motor slowly towards the pass.

Robin takes the wheel and they stand at attention. They know the importance of this moment, of this passage from the still, lethargic lagoon to the ocean. The boat rides rough over the swell in the pass, breakers to either side, but the engine holds true and strong.

They have reached the open ocean, and do not look back.

*L*ucy felt the lively motion of the boat as a tightness of both fear and excitement at the back of her throat. She stood by Robin in the cockpit and watched the waves, gauging their height and the strength of the wind. It was a mild day, but it seemed rough after the tranquillity of the island.

"I think we can use the big drifter," said Robin, "what do you say? There's not much wind yet."

She nodded at his choice of sail. "I'll go get it."

The sails were kept in a walk-in locker in the very bow of the boat, beyond the forward cabin. They also kept spare line, tools, and parts there. Lucy made her way forward, waddling with the motion of the boat, then braced herself against the bunk to pull the locker door open. Yet she found that however she tugged, the door was stuck fast and she could not open it. She went back on deck.

"The door's stuck—with the heat, I suppose. I'll take the wheel, you try."

Robin reappeared some minutes later, trailing a mass of colorful sailcloth.

"I didn't have any trouble," he called, "except that the drifter wasn't in its bag. What a mess."

"Did you find the bag?"

"No. We'll look later."

Lucy remained at the wheel while Robin went forward to hank on the sail. She thrilled to the motion of the boat as it danced along the swell, spray bursting towards the bow; she did not want to think of what lay behind them and its puzzling ambiguity. There would be time enough for that—for now the day was lovely, the sky a baby's blanket dotted with fleecy clouds.

Robin joined her at the wheel. The sail was ready to be raised. He stood for a moment with his arm around her, sharing the boat's forward surge. He felt that now they were together again, sailing true and free.

"I'll raise the sail, head up a bit for now," he told her, and started forward.

But he never made it, because at that moment the engine moaned, and slowed, as if it would die, then grunted and popped and rose again. Robin looked at Lucy with horror, as she did at him, and they knew what this meant.

Robin hurried back to the wheel, gave some throttle, listened, watched, then shook his head, slowing the engine as he did so.

"It's not good. What do you think?"

"Oh, Robin, we've got wind—can't we keep going?"

"I think I know what it is. I think I can fix it fairly quickly. We should turn back right away, while we still have slack water. We're so close."

"Oh, can't we sail, for God's sake?"

"Of course we can sail, but then what? Do you really want to take the chance, to try to get into an unknown harbor, past all those reefs, without an engine? Let's just go back now while it's slack water and fix it. Now, out of my way."

Robin swung the wheel about and set *Stowaway* on her course back to the island. For something to do, and to relieve her disappointment, Lucy removed the flapping drifter from the headstay and carried it below, in a crumpled heap, into the storage room. The bow of the boat was now pointing towards the calmer waters of the pass, between the walls of breaking waves. It was so easy to see the pass, this time. How could they have made such a grave mistake that day?

They do not speak as they enter the lagoon. The island has not changed, but its familiarity makes it different. There is now an uneasy sense of homecoming.

*

Robin does not begin work that afternoon, but pores over engine manuals, notes, reference books. He must think, let it sink in, he tells Lucy, as if referring to an intellectual, not practical, problem. Dejected, she lies on her bunk reading detective stories. The windows of Scotland Yard look out onto a cold, wet, gray world, one where she would like to be.

After dark, after a hurried meal, they lie in their cabin, the hatch open upon a square of night sky. They are tired from their failed effort to leave, tired with discouragement.

"Are you upset?" he asks gently.

"I suppose. I wanted to be on our way . . . out of here. I feel more trapped here than ever, now."

"Perhaps we are trapped. Perhaps there's an evil genie on the island who will never let us leave." He laughs softly.

"You mean the ghost. Whenever we turn our backs he pours sugar into the diesel."

"You mean sand. He hasn't got sugar."

"No, of course." She sighs and curls up against him.

"But seriously," she continues, "don't you ever feel events are conspiring against you . . . as if things are just not meant to happen the way you would like them to?"

"All the time."

"And?"

"You can't fight it. It only makes it worse."

"So does that mean you shouldn't repair the engine, for example?"

"No, it's not that . . . it means that you need to change your way of looking, that you have to take a different attitude, and it will all come clear."

"For example?"

"Well, instead of thinking that the most important thing is to repair the engine, and be out of here, perhaps we should think that the most important thing is *being* here—there is a reason for being here that only the future will reveal."

"Like the ghost." She laughs.

"No, I'm serious—we have to make more of being here, find out *why* we're here."

"We're here because we're stuck here," she insists.

He shrugs and begins to rub her shoulder with his thumb, idly, softly, as if to polish it. Her shoulder catches the moonlight as the boat swings gently at anchor; he feels as if he is rubbing the light into her skin.

Later, as they sleep beneath their patch of open sky with its web of silvered light, Lucy is woken by a noise. She cannot trace its source, since she has been asleep, but as she lies staring at nothing, confronting her sudden apprehension, she hears another sound outside the hull. Faint gurgles, splashing, a swimming sound. She is about to wake Robin, then thinks better of it. It must be that stupid shark, checking us out, she reasons.

The sound grows fainter, and does not return.

In the morning Robin is back at work on the engine and Lucy remembers the untidy drifter in the storage room. She goes forward and opens the door; when she looks for the sail she finds it has already been stowed in its bag.

Bless his heart, she thinks; he finds time to do everything.

$\mathcal{I}$t was the laughter.

They stood on the beach where I had left their small boat; he muttered something, she laughed—a clear, chiming arpeggio; then he joined her and I was alone in laughless isolation.

The laughter carried them across the water to their home; the laughter reached deep into my indecision. I wanted to call, to shout—wait, I'll come with you after all, one last grand adventure, a twilight of shared laughter. Let it peal, ring, boom out over the ocean—with you, all of us together. Time must allow me that: I must have laughter.

I waited until they were belowdecks, then swam into my future. Across the concentric circles of their laughter I paddled my tired body, the fatigue growing as I left the shore. I did not stop to think, I did not meditate on the heaviness of my decision. I did not look at the island behind me. I saw only my brilliant future, when I would be restored to my own kind. My triumphant arrival: "End of a Mystery," "Return from the Dead," "She Sails Back to Fame"—the trumpet of tabloids.

The lagoon became a vast mirror to my vanity.

I waited, hiding in the lee of the hull, listening. Then I crept aboard at the bow, climbing first into the small boat which had, indirectly, been the cause of this sudden decision. The sailboat rocked, very gently, as I pulled myself on deck, timing my effort to meet the natural swell of the lagoon; I was prepared to jump into the water should they discover me. I was not yet ready to meet them.

I could hear music from the main cabin, and quiet laughter. I looked into the hatch by the bow: there was a double berth where they must sleep, and just forward of it was a small door.

I dropped through the hatch and tried the door. It opened into a large cupboard full of sails where I might hide until I was ready to come out, or until they found me. The door had a latch, I could lock it from the inside. I did this, then curled up on the sails to wait.

I felt very weak. I had not felt like this for many years, so I blamed the exertion. I laughed silently at my vanity and looked down at my hands. In the dim light which came in through a vent in the door they were brown and wrinkled, a crone's hands, covered with spots. Of course I should feel tired, at my age! The heat in the small cabin was suffocating. It was the first time I had been truly indoors for so many years. I felt dizzy and shut my eyes; the room closed around me, hot and dark and airless.

I slept. In my dream a large metal plate like the flank of an airplane was pressing down upon my lungs, pinching breath from me. I was returning to earth from the sky, but I did not see fields of green and gold or spired villages; I did not see the regular sunscrubbed ripples of the sea. I saw a deep-gray surging flood around me—no sky, no earth, only this thick gray impenetrable liquid. I was pinned among other struggling bodies, strangers with open mouths, their eyes staring fishlike. I could not swim, or walk, I could only make a weak pedaling motion with my feet, and each time I moved, my body was racked with a deep, dull pain I perceived as electrocution, or drowning death itself.

I awoke drenched in sweat. On the island I did not sweat, ever; I knew the cool places, the cool moments. I had forgotten sweat.

The boat was moving, up and down, like a merry-go-round. The engine vibrated.

Someone tried to come into the sail room. The small door shook and rattled, the handle bobbed. I waited until they left, then dumped the largest sail from its bag onto the pile, unlocked the door, and crawled into the empty bag. What a fine pickle, for my glorious return to the world, to be trussed up like a rabbit in a pouch.

Shortly afterward the man came into the room—I could hear him cursing as he gathered the sail into his arms. I lay cramped and breathless in my blue bag. He was surely a kind man—why was I so afraid of discovery?

Because I could not let go of the island. Because it was still there, just beyond the hull, the reef, the lagoon, and my life was there, on the island. My spirit had stayed behind, and this thing stowed away in a sailbag was not my self, but a mere bundle of bones and flesh, oozing sweat, tossed upon a sea I was never meant to cross.

What had I done? How had I allowed myself to be tricked by their laughter—as if there were a place for me there?

I had been free on the island, and only now did I realize it. For the first forty years my life had not been my own but that of an uncommon woman who belonged to the world—to both her admirers and detractors, to all those who lived, through her, those great adventures. (Did some part of them die when she failed to return?)

What part of me, in these last forty years, was brought to life when I learned to listen, through the patient guidance of the island, to the nascent singing of my soul?

It was a heavy exchange, their adulation for my unheard, very private music.

I could not go back to them. Although they would know of me and I would fill their newspapers and radio broadcasts and newsreels once again for a few days, they would then tire of me and leave me—an old woman, a curiosity, a stranger.

I was no stranger to the island. How could I have betrayed it, and myself?

Sometime later the big sail was dumped in upon me, unused. Something was wrong; the engine was making strange, sick noises.

The boat bounced and turned; before long a smoother motion told me that we were back in the lagoon. Soon there followed the rattle of the anchor chain, just above my head; then silence.

I am now in almost total darkness. I am weary, but I struggle to put the sail back in its bag. Why I do it, I do not know. A guest's politeness, a ghost's playfulness. I lie in my hot cell and listen to the murmur of voices from the bed next door. Murmurs, soft laughter, whispers, sweet moans.

I lie and listen to this music of the heart and it fills me with sadness. To stay on this boat and go with them in search of what they have—it is too late, I am too old. To swim ashore and return to the shelter—there I will lie and listen to my own memories, perhaps to defeat time once again and bring past joy into the present.

Like a thief in the night, I creep past the sleeping couple and steal from the boat with my future, to swim through a lagoon strewn with moonlight. The night air pulses with perfume; I am part of the night. Part of the island, I step ashore and its warmth enfolds me, welcoming.

*I*sland. Let me think of you, in me.

I lie here on the sand at Desolation Cove. Noddies and petrels circle; I wonder at my madness. To have left the island—or to choose, this time, to stay. Some deeply buried prejudice from my up- bringing, from my childhood, tells me I must attempt to return to so- ciety, even if it means my death; the island whispers to me of a life beyond death, and of the eternal beauty of the present. We have no words in our language for this knowledge of a life outside time.

I am afraid that if I returned to that other world I would lose the beauty and the meaning of this life. How could I explain to anyone what it means, if I have no words?

Who would listen to an old woman?

But, by staying here, there is no old woman. There are no wrin- kles, no lines, no sad wasting of the flesh. No judgment, no pity, no indifference.

I see only a sentient being in a body touched with the grace of be- longing.

The sun beats on my skin and the heat is terrible, but the wind lays a cool hand upon me, the caress of a lover. If it rains, I am soaked through and cold; then the sun returns, to warm me this time like a welcome fire, and the cycle is complete.

The elements are my lover. I press my body into the sand.

Sometimes I touch myself as lovers touched me. It is a gift in my body to know pleasure, but a sadness to know it alone. Sometimes the pleasure comes to me in sleep and then I awake with a sweet well-being: my body has sung on its own, without the stern choir- master of the mind's desire.

*

The mind has not always been so easily contented. There were long hours, days, of boredom when we first came to the island. I had to play games, with Fred: ticktacktoe in the sand, chess with primitive hand-made figurines. Later, I had to make up my own solitary games. To pass the time.

One day I understood, after Kuma had gone and I lay watching the passing of the clouds, that to "pass" the time is wrong; a terrible ailment once afflicted me, still afflicts, perhaps, those among whom I once lived. I wanted to skip over time until something took me away from myself (a radio broadcast from the president, a play at the theater, a night in company). That was wrong because I deprived myself of the present, when I should have been watching the clouds, or thinking about the watching of clouds.

There is no word for my state of grace on the island; we invented the word for time, and in so doing, invented time itself and lost that state of grace.

Animals sit quietly in the sun, under the large sky. They watch, they feel, in their way they think, with their other sense of which we know so little. They are better adapted to the present; one wonders if they know of past or future.

I learn to sit like an animal, my pores open to the necessity of life. The earth smells ripe and rich of existence.

I have my memories, too. I lie in the sand or on my pallet and they come to me, changing cumulus on the sky of the past.

In dreams memories are transformed and become reality. If I cannot touch those visions with my meddling thoughts, if my sleeping mind and body perceive them as reality, then surely that makes them so. Thus I am still able to fly. And to crash-land upon awakening.

At times the pain of wakefulness is great, with the sharpness of memories, sleeping lions, disturbed. Then I must fight for forgetful-

ness and serenity in the beauty of the present. I go into the lagoon and release my pain to the cerulean hues of its depths; I lie undisturbed on the glass-smooth water. Even the sharks fear the sharpness of my pain.

The ocean brings me its gifts. Not just the shells, the driftwood, the fine-ground colored pieces of glass; it also brings me the detritus of civilization. I wonder that man has produced so much, that his castoffs can travel to me, almost daily, on my remote island, and he cannot.

Bottles, cans, containers printed with Japanese characters; drawers with handles (whose hands?); huge salt-ravaged lengths of timber; jagged rusty sides of metal; shiny bags made of a strange stretchy material. Tokens of a world I do not know.

Once I found a huge conch shell, big and pink as a melon. I listened: in it I heard, not the sea, but the drone of propellers.

*L*ucy decides to row ashore. Since they have been called back to the island, it must be for a reason, Robin said; there must be more to learn, to discover.

Robin is glum and silent. He is not angry with her but she leaves him apologetically, almost regretfully. His squatting pose by the engine is too familiar. She knows the meaning of the almost visible tension of muscles in his neck.

The sky has changed. The clouds are thickening, mackerel-sky, towards an opaque cover. The island is washed with a flat light; there are no shadows, no ladders of light in the palm groves. Lucy would like rain. They could wash, do laundry, top up their water supply—just in case they have been imagining things. She is not sure how well Robin can read the level on the tank; perhaps he has been mistaken.

She walks idly, with no destination in mind. There is no destination on this island, she thinks; no purpose, no intended arrival. So she strolls, watching for wildlife, waiting for her thoughts to rise like mist from a pond.

She is disappointed that they have had to come back, but not really surprised. She wants to doubt the reliability of things like engines—breakdown seems inevitable, innate. Manufacturers build in the various stages of obsolescence; when one decides to replace rather than repair yet again is a question of personal choice, or circumstances. But she also doubts the reliability of her faith in Robin. She keeps trying to believe, he keeps failing her—or is it she who is failing? Does she not know how to keep her faith alive? Is this to say that obsolescence is built into marriage, too?

Now there is the fear of pregnancy, the fear that Robin will have another hold over her or that the marriage will continue on false premises. She has known parents who stayed together because of their children; she suspects her own parents did so. The house was always full of brooding silences and unspoken griev-ances; on her wedding day her mother said to her, "I hope you'll be happy, dear," as if the foregone conclusion was that she would not. Happy, in any case, was the wrong word; contentment, yes, one could reasonably strive for contentment.

Is she, has she been, content? Lucy stops, throws her head back, breathes deeply the changing air. Yes, she has been content, but she worries now about the future. Worries that some invisible reef will close around her, cutting off the pass, leaving her stranded in a too blue lagoon of illusions.

She has wound her way south along the lagoon; now she joins the eastern beach at its southernmost tip and begins to head north.

The wind has picked up. It pushes small leaves, twigs and bits of scrub across her path. There are whitecaps beyond the reef. This is real weather—they have not seen real weather since they left the West Coast of America. Only relentless blue sky, the occasional cinematographic clouds, a few sudden tropical downpours in Hawaii. This feels real and vaguely menacing; perhaps she should return to the boat.

She is about to turn when something causes her to look to one side—imagination, hallucination, reality?

By the shore at the little cove a woman sits, her legs crossed, looking out to the ocean. She wears a much-faded plaid shirt; a long white braid reaches down her back into the sand. Lucy can-not see her face. She hesitates—should she approach, speak to her? But then, suddenly, the woman is on her feet. A cry parts her lips as she rushes forward into the water. Did she say, come back? Is she sobbing, still, come back, as she fights her way deeper into the water?

Lucy looks away, panicked. When she looks back, only a few seconds later, the woman is gone.

She approaches the place where the woman was sitting, to look for a trace, a proof of what she has seen. But there is nothing, only myriad silent grains of sand.

Later, she does not tell Robin what she has or has not seen. How can she be sure of such a thing?

Robin is depressed. He is once again getting nowhere with the engine. He does everything by the book, carefully, meticulously, and still the engine coughs and dies. He lacks some vital inspiration, or detachment. He cares too much.

He tells Lucy this over supper; she seems preoccupied too, in need of company.

"Why don't you take two days off? Just *stop working*. Read, come for walks . . ."

He nods. "I'm tired; perhaps I'm not thinking straight."

There is a sound on deck, surprising and welcome. Robin looks at her; she smiles. The sound of raindrops.

They go up into the twilight and stand watching, listening, feeling. They hold each other and feel it run from one to the other: the cool dampness. Like a welcome forgiveness.

The next day they leave the boat, early, and take a picnic to the island. The air is fresh and bright from the light rainfall of the night before. They find a shady grove; they spread their towels beneath them. They read, then, when they are hungry, Lucy takes their lunch from the canvas bag. Homemade bread, some olives, canned meat, potato salad, canned pears. Robin opens a rare bottle of red wine, saved for just such an occasion.

The wine leaves them heavy with warmth and drowsiness. They push the luncheon things aside, and Robin curls up against Lucy's back. He lifts her hair, kisses the nape of her neck. It is moist with heat.

She presses back against him. "Take off my shirt," she murmurs. She lies there like a cat, taking his caresses, drifting between sleep and contentment.

The problem with our marriage, thinks Lucy, later, as they walk back to the dinghy, the problem is that we do not have enough moments like that, of spontaneity, sensuality, abandon. We run on rails, we don't know how to get off, so we speed on through, everything becoming a blur of the half-seen, the half-felt. We miss the richness of the wayside.

Even when sailing we thrust ourselves into the practicalities, the daily difficulties of the boat's performance, and we do not see each other.

When did it happen? When did it become easier to turn to habit for guidance? When did we lose our special vision?

$\mathcal{M}$y curiosity is not good for me—I have let it get the better of me, and now I must pay a price.

They went ashore this morning; I went to their boat, yet again. I want to learn what it can tell me of the world I left. Now that I do not mean to return, I thought that such knowledge could not harm me, that it would only confirm me in my decision to stay on my ungoverned island. But what I have found disturbs me because it confirms only my loneliness and isolation, and calls my decision into question.

I did not stay long on the boat. I did not take water this time. I think they have enough for a while. Nor did I try the ship's radio—what would be the point? But I took some things I hoped they would not miss, things which they can replace, because they can go back; I can only go on.

I took some food: a packet of rice. A jar of raspberry jam, a jar of peanut butter: these I eat with my fingers, greedily, voluptuously. But the tastes assault my palate—too rich, too sweet. Then there is a packet of something which looks like bird food, full of grains and seeds, but it tastes of cinnamon, and reminds me of childhood, of oatmeal sprinkled with cinnamon on cold winter mornings when Pidge and I had been sledding in new-fallen snow. The immediacy of memory, the power of sensation to defy time.

I did not know when they would return to the boat. Sometimes they stay on the island for hours, sometimes only minutes. In addition to a news magazine—one I used to read! not much changed on the outside—and food, I grabbed a few more books and some blank paper, quickly, from the shelf near the companionway.

I am disappointed in my haste. The books are mostly about sailing, practical books. Of no use to me on my motionless island. I will have to return them.

*

There is my past, and the past of the world; both are gone, behind me, but still they reach into the present, trying to draw me back. I have read the news magazine twice, slowly; I am puzzled by what it tells me, what I can infer from what is left out—that which I am supposed to know.

There is talk of Kuma's great war, and I am confused. He told me the Japanese had been defeated, but the magazine does not speak of Japan as of a defeated nation. The world has been rearranged, once again, and instead of one Germany there are now two. Is that good? I remember the menace, the horrible stories of persecution we heard. But there is no mention of Hitler or the thousand-year Reich; "West" Germany, like Japan, is doing very well exporting automobiles, says the article. But the persecution goes on elsewhere; now in Cambodia where, I read, thousands are being massacred. And this note: "In 1973, American bombers dropped on Cambodia a tonnage of bombs equivalent to five Hiroshimas." What does this mean? What happened in Hiroshima—was it the great bomb Kuma spoke of? How could America do this to Cambodia, then, and why? And what is this horrible genocide there, despite bombs? What of France—was Cambodia not part of Indochina? (I had flown so close, I could see the shores in the distance, bathing their magic in the Gulf of Siam . . .)

The French, I read further on, are testing nuclear bombs in the South Pacific—is it far from here? Are they now the most powerful nation on earth, with this horrible new weapon of destruction?

Oh, I am glad for my island at this time.

But I read also of a "birth-control pill" and the "feminist movement," and this heartens me somewhat, for perhaps it means that if the human race has not acquired much sense in forty years, at least things are better for women now. There is a Mrs. Gandhi, who has been Prime Minister of India and who is trying to be reelected. Such a vast nation—what has happened to the British? To think, a woman has replaced the British!

Most intriguing of all is a passing reference to the "Tenth anniversary of the moon landing." I look in vain for any explanation or clarification.

I do not know what to believe in what I read, what part is truth and what part is only what I must conclude in my ignorance. This solitary magazine is a very powerful thing in my aroused imagination—but what relevance does any of it have for me?

Only that I will look, now, at the moon with questioning—its face, though unchanged, will now and forever reflect my isolation, my unanswered questions.

The sailboat is very quiet these days. No sounds of engine, no movement on deck. Once I heard music across the lagoon, faint and delicate.

I believe it was Mozart's Clarinet Concerto. How did they play it? I sat and listened and felt the melancholy strains of the Adagio like a pain from within: pain for the music itself, pain for the forty years I have heard no music created by man.

In lonely moments I used to sit with my eyes closed and try to re-create music in my head. I could remember many of the symphonies, concertos, even operas; but this hearing in my mind frustrated me, left me with a deep longing not for the pale uncertain echo of the New World Symphony as I imagined it, but for the real, vibrant sound, even as poorly reproduced by the radio or the gramophone. Some music simply faded from my mind in mid-refrain, forgotten; for days I would try to pick up the thread of the melody, then gradually it would all fade away, leaving the resonance of the birds, the surf, the wind, once again.

*L*ucy, in her restlessness, asks Robin to go ashore to take a sun sight. They will take the sextant to a point on the island where there is an unobstructed horizon, then they will return and, using the almanac and tables, gratefully undisturbed by waves or haste, they will calculate their position.

Robin carries the sextant in its lacquered box. Lucy holds a timepiece, pen and pad. They walk to the southernmost point of the island to catch the sun at its zenith. Robin enjoys navigation. It is a science, despite the variables which can make it anything but exact. There is something awe-inspiring about being able to capture the sun in a trick of lenses and mirrors, to stare at it freely through darkened filters, to bring it down onto the horizon in order to find one's position and say, we are here, in this little quadrant of ocean. Rolling the sun down the sky: sleight of hand, power of ingenuity over Nature.

He calls degrees and minutes and seconds of arc to Lucy; she scribbles the figures down with the time. Over and over they bob the sun to the horizon; for fairness, Lucy also swings the arc. When they are sure that noon is well past and that the sun is beginning its own, true, downward roll, they pack the sextant and head for home.

But when Lucy gathers the tables and worksheets from the navigation table to begin reducing the sight, she cannot find the nautical almanac. She questions Robin, a note of irritation in her voice; he was the last to use it, trying to correct her eighty-miles-out sight. He rebukes her for excessive, obsessive tidiness, for always putting things away beyond retrieval.

They search everywhere—upending lockers, emptying shelves, but the almanac is not there. Robin rants; Lucy broods. It is vitally important for their navigation; they will not be able to determine their position on the chart without it.

*

Robin returns to the engine, glum but resigned. Lucy continues to brood. There is more he does not know about. Her period is now definitely overdue. It is not cause for immediate alarm; it often happens when she is upset, when their routine is broken. But possibility and uncertainty continue to nag, urging her towards pharmacies, towards knowledge she thinks the island cannot give her.

The season is changing; there have been suggestions of the equatorial winter storms to come. Westerly winds, ponderous clouds, which will return, soon, bearing more rain. Six days after their false start they are no closer to leaving the lagoon.

"I'm giving you a deadline," says Lucy one evening. "If you haven't fixed the engine by the end of this week, whenever that is, we use the dinghy and outboard to get ourselves out of the lagoon and do the same in Betio. I don't care how dangerous you think the pass is. I think staying here is more dangerous. Right?"

Robin nods without looking, without speaking. As a sailor he dare not underestimate the fury of the waters in the pass. The odds of finding a favorable wind to sail out, or a mild current through which to tow the boat—he knows they are slim, and foolishly reckoned. But he must humor her; he has begun to feel he is living on borrowed time.

Sometimes Robin goes up on deck, alone, and looks out to the pass where *Stowaway* was almost lost. The breakers seem to grow higher as he watches, louder, menacing, a clashing chorus of sirens telling him he will never escape, he is doomed to stay. His fear rises because he knows they must escape, and because he has allowed his imagination to cast him onto the reef, again and again. Once, while Lucy sleeps, he takes the dinghy to the pass to become acquainted with his fear. The tide is ebbing; the waters swirl and boil in the narrow gap between the treacherous breakwaters of the reef. He rides out on the dinghy, surfing and twisting on the foam; only by pushing the outboard to its maximum speed is he able to cross the current back into the lagoon.

Lucy's ultimatum is unreasonable. Dangerous, even at slack water. How can he make her understand both the logic of this and his own fear? They must leave the island with the engine.

Two days go by. The engine fires and misses, spurts and dies. If Robin could shed tears of frustration, he would. Instead he watches Lucy banging around the galley, her tears of frustration running free down her cheeks as she fails to find the last jar of raspberry jam. "I'm so sick of this, so sick of being stuck here and nothing goes right and I can't even enjoy a jar of fucking *jam!*"

He leaves his tools, climbs out of the engine room and puts his arms around her, carefully keeping his oil-stained hands away from her white T-shirt. She resists briefly, then relents; he whispers a suggestion to her.

Moments later they are in the dinghy, rowing ashore through a fresh breeze. They have some cookies and canned fruit and a flask of juice. They pull the dinghy high up on the beach; for precaution's sake Robin now ties the rope to the base of the nearest palm tree.

They disappear into the heart of the island, hand in hand.

This is good, thinks Lucy, as she rolls towards Robin, as his hands mold her and define her pleasure. We lie here naked beneath an awning of palm leaves; the sun can barely find its way to us. The breeze in its freshness is more tender and sensuous than our own caresses, if that is possible.

When they return, hours later, to the dinghy, the rope is not tied to the same tree. Robin looks at Lucy and wonders whether he is merely imagining things, whether she has noticed; she wonders whether to tell him about the woman she saw. But she hesitates, uncertain of her own imagination: perhaps it was herself that she saw, some dreamlike incarnation of her own lonely future. She cannot tease Robin with figments and mirages, his scientific mind will not accept what she says. So she says nothing.

But it is Robin, when they return to the boat, who now suggests a presence on the island, saying, quite emphatically and with no explanation, "Someone has been on the boat."

"What makes you say that?"

"Look."

Sitting on the shelf in its usual place by the navigation table is the familiar orange-and-black nautical almanac for 1979.

Robin becomes obsessed with the idea of a silent, stealthy islander toying with their possessions, violating their sovereignty. He says little but as he works, more feverishly determined than ever, he sees dark limbs climb aboard to finger their books and clothes and jam; eyes watch him and his wife as they touch and make love on the island. His anger rises until he can no longer stand not knowing, not acting. Late the next afternoon he puts his tools away and turns to Lucy. "I'm stiff. I'm going back to the island for a run. You'll stay here?"

She nods, grateful for some time alone. She senses his irritation and does not want to be caught in its rays. She waves as, aided by a brisk westerly breeze, he rows ashore.

"Don't be long!" she calls, "the sun's nearly down."

"Don't worry! Just a quick run around the island."

Lucy goes below and sits on her berth with her notebook. Her thoughts are restless and will not form themselves on the page, but rather dart and jump from the paper to her mind. Could there indeed be someone on the island, so clever, so Indian-quiet that he could defy detection for so long? But then they know nothing of the aboriginal skills of the islanders or of their possible fear of detection.

She scribbles in her notebook:

> Shipwrecked? Castaway? Ostracized for some reason—madman, leper, murderer?
>
> The old white woman I thought I saw? Anthropologist eccentric, on a grant from Stanford University?

The boat rocks her to sleep. She dreams of the woman with the long white braid. She sees her creeping away from the berth, at first only a disembodied white braid; then the woman turns. She has a kind face, neither old nor young, and she is holding a baby up to Lucy, nodding speechlessly, as if to say, "Well, do you want it? Take it, it's yours!"

In her dream Lucy is frightened, by both the strange woman and the baby. She wakes suddenly, with relief, before making a decision. Her heart is pounding; the light in the cabin is dim, but it is not yet dark outside. Robin will be back soon, she will wait for him to wake her. She drifts away again, into a different, dreamless sleep.

Robin runs across the island, then up the beach, pausing now and again to listen. He hears nothing but the thump of his own heart, his heat-burdened breathing. He sees nothing but what he is sure are his and Lucy's footprints from the previous day. Mindless of cuts and scratches, he pushes through undergrowth they have always avoided. He finds nothing.

But when he returns to the dinghy, he finds on the thwart a perfectly shaped bowl made from a coconut shell, full of fresh coconut water. He lifts the bowl and hurls it out into the lagoon; drops dissolve into the sand before the shell lands in the water, where it sits bobbing like a small boat in a quiet harbor.

"I can't stand it. There's someone here and they're bloody clever at hiding behind trees and playing silly games."

Lucy says nothing as he paces up and down the short space of their saloon.

"I'm not leaving until we find that . . . jam thief," he exclaims.

"Don't be daft! I'm not staying here just so you can terrorize some poor islander who's on his own land, just trying to offer something in exchange for the jam."

"And what about my paperback? He never brought that back! A college-educated islander?"

"It's probably on the boat, we've never looked properly . . . Look, can't you just finish this damned engine so we can get out of here?"

"No, I *want* to find that nosy bastard, and I'll not leave here until I do."

"Well, then you can stay here by yourself with him and I'll take the bloody boat to Betio."

"Like hell you will! Fat lot you've done to try and find this stupid ghost that scares *you* so and eats *your* fucking jam!"

Lucy waits to hear no more but rushes up the ladder, out the hatch, over the lifelines and into the dinghy. Her first strokes hit the water with the flat of the oar, splashing water wildly, furious and uneven. Then, slowly, the motion calms her, she is gliding, away; she is rowing towards the island where there are no words that can hurt her, no sound beyond the muttering of the trees, the wind, the sea.

I did not mean to anger him. It was an offering, *Ko na mauri.* I could make it so easy for him, I could come out and show myself, but I do not trust him. He would have me go with him and be his hostage to fame. "The Man Who Found . . ." Et cetera. No. So I let him run and sweat in his quest, and I try to ease his thirst at the end of it all. An ironic gesture from a sly old woman, after all.

All that running, like a rat in a cage. For him that is what this island must be. A place where he is caught until his science can triumph over the stubbornness of someone else's machinery; he is caught by the urgency of departure, as if this island were not good enough. He wants to raise his sails and flit from place to place like a moth in a lamp shop. I was like that once, too.

Now the girl Lucy is here, and her face is a red, scowling glow in the late-afternoon sun. She is angry; they have quarreled. She marches along the beach to the far end of the lagoon, far from her boat. Then she lies in the sand and stares into the sky, her arms tossed behind her head. And she begins to cry. Loudly, without shame, in the comfort of solitude.

She cries but I cannot pity her. I too know something of tears.

I sit and watch her until dark, beyond dark, into a night first black, then washed with silver like the negative of a film, as the moon rises. I watch her beyond dark and she does not know she is being watched. I see her anger and her sadness. She pounds the sand with her fist, then buries her head in her arms. I do not know the story in her head, in her heart, as she rocks herself on the sand or hangs her head on her knees.

I could tell her a story.

The sea took him and left me, too strong, to carry the burden of memory.

*

We had been on the island for six months or so. It seemed a very long time; we had quickly exhausted those reserves of patience which had enabled us to while away the time, always looking, always hoping. We had played the old games to saturation: chess, ticktacktoe, checkers, battleships—whatever we could fabricate or invent. After a time the mere idea of another game was a boredom in itself. So we had turned apart—not through any animosity towards each other, really, but because we knew we would also have to explore separate, private paths of existence in order to keep from going mad.

Fred spent a lot of time fishing. It seemed to absorb him so easily. I had always marveled at men's capacity to sit or stand for so long while fishing quietly, waiting, all attention focused on the whim of another creature's hunger. But he was so good at it. He could never explain it, perhaps was not even aware of it in this way, but I think he lost all sense of time when he was fishing; his concentration was so great, our own need for survival so present, that it freed him from the confines of time—of waiting, of feeling imprisoned on the island.

I did not have that gift. I envied him his fishing and had to hide my envy. I tried it myself for a while but did not have his patience and therefore failed to catch anything. I sometimes came along when he was spearfishing; I surprised myself, guiltily, hoping for a shark to appear to add some excitement to my day, to take Fred away from his state of timelessness and force him, at least, to share my frustration.

I tried so hard with my poetry. But that, too, failed me at times; I was mute without an audience, buried in my own head, deafened by my own voice. He tried a few times to listen; he would cock his head to one side, then say, "Very pretty, very nice," before standing up, abruptly, to move on to something else. My poems were to him as his fish were to me, but incapable, even, of nourishing him.

There were times I thought I would go mad, listening to silence.

But as Fred navigated us through the difficulties of our primitive life I was his willing passenger. Some atavistic drive to provide food and shelter became the focus of his existence, something in which he could take pride. I acknowledged his capabilities, gratefully; I accepted his newly acquired ascendancy. I could no longer pilot him or fly above him; my capabilities had been of another era.

He fished while I wrote poetry; then I cooked while he whittled his useful, artistic things. We did not talk a great deal; memories were painful to both of us, and philosophizing about our predicament did not bring much comfort. There was a natural reserve and an ironic politeness in our behavior, a residue of our former professional relationship.

But his sense of humor led us to a place where we could see release from our struggle, a freedom of a kind, like a patch of blue torn in the clouds. Dry and witty, almost imperceptible at times, this humor was perhaps a legacy of the war years he had spent in His Majesty's navy, or perhaps merely a natural trait of his Irish background. Hardship, he showed me, could be defeated by only one thing: humor. If you could still laugh and make fun of your own misfortune, you were in with a chance against the devil trying to get you down.

He had me laughing at the antics of seabirds or crabs, at our own difficulties preparing a certain fish for the fire, at leaks in the shelter during a midwinter downpour. He had me laughing at myself.

The hardship is long gone, but then so is the laughter: real, deep, soul-releasing laughter.

*

One day I was walking among the trees, searching for any edible flowers or plants (this was long before the hibiscus, the frangipani, the banana trees), when I heard Fred calling from far away, towards the lagoon. There was an excitement in his voice, a jubilation, which could mean only one thing. I began to run, despite heat and prickly things at my feet, to run towards that hope in his voice.

There, perhaps three miles to the southwest of the island, slowly steaming, was a ship.

We built the biggest bonfire we could muster in so short a time: all the dry scrub and grasses burned bright to hasten our liberation. We thought we would set the island ablaze with our eagerness to be gone and our contempt for its keyless jailer.

We stood and watched. The ship replied, three short blasts on its horn.

Yes, we cried, they've seen us, we're free, we're free, and as on that long-ago day when our captivity began but survival was our victory, we fell into each other's arms, dancing, hugging, swinging.

"This is it, Captain," he said quietly, giving me a small squeeze of rare tenderness. "We'll be home soon. Home."

I closed my eyes and pictured it, impossibly beautiful. Then it faded, suddenly and unexpectedly, and I looked at Fred, so close, still holding me. He was strong and muscled by work, honed by our basic, meager diet and browned by the sun. For the first time I noticed his arms, his brown chest in his worn cotton singlet; for the first time I noticed my own body, thin and pale underneath my brown plaid shirt, and sticky with heat. Our skin, where it touched, seemed to cling. He was smiling at me, but looking at the ship. We stood for a long time like that and we watched the black smoke funneling into the sky. Again I tried to think of home, but saw only the smoke and the dark skin of his arms.

Then his hands were holding my arms, he was pushing me,

gently, away. "They're going by," he muttered. "They're not stop-ping."

"Oh no, God, they've got to, Fred, we've got to stop them; we can do something, we must, come on!" I ran to the water's edge, I shouted, jumped, prayed that someone would be standing on the bridge, watching with binoculars; I ran to the life raft and began to drag it across the sand, I would row after them, they would see me, they had to—

"Stop it, it's no good, don't . . ."

He put his hand against the rubber raft and looked up at me, the only look left on earth, the deepness of his eyes, a well, a world, all the sadness in the world. We collapsed against the raft; we needed no more tears, we were surrounded by a vast ocean, empty once again.

How long did we stay like that, flung against the agonizing im-age of a ship retreating beyond our reach? I remember the terrible heat of the day, then the gradual cooling of sunset, then a night full of stars, like hundreds of nights gone by, and hundreds, per-haps thousands, more to come, unchanging. We could learn the fantastic weave of the stars' tapestry, but we could never again navigate by them. Only the stars could move for us—predictably, in an ordered universe.

Thus were we ordered to stay on our little orbit: sleep, rise, co-conuts, fish and poetry, walking, more fish and poetry, sleep. What we did not know at the time was that the ship was to give us something after all. A gift to be revealed slowly, to the rhythm of those same stars circling in the night.

We were very quiet for some days after the ship's passing. We shared the same sense of loss, but our thoughts were of our respec-tive families, our separate lives, and to speak together was only to remind each other of who, or where, we were not.

But he was there, Fred, and he was different. Or I saw him differently. Or something in me had begun to change, from the moment we saw the ship. This tall skinny sunbaked bearded man was no longer the Navigator with whom I had tried to circle the globe; nor was he the castaway who fished and whittled and swore when he thought I could not hear him. He was the Other One, the only person left in my dwindled universe, the only creature who could feel, and think, and share. And, I thought, our great loneliness and eagerness to be gone from the island was due, in part, to our failure to see each other.

And when this vision changed, everything began to change.

He became moody. A terse "I'll be back, see you later," was followed by hours of absence and brooding silence upon his return. I asked him once where he went; he answered, evasively, "Oh, here and there," as if he had been to the post office, then the cleaner's, then finally the bar.

Nor could I explain my heightened interest in his absence, or presence. When he was there, whittling, whistling, humming to himself, I observed him, as if his activity were part of a film or a book, a story for my entertainment. His long, thin fingers were a pleasure to me, moving as if of their own accord as he fashioned a spoon or a flat, dull-bladed knife. From time to time he caught me looking at him; once he said, "Why so sad, Captain?"

I shrugged and smiled. "I'm not sad."

"Then don't look at me like that."

"Like what?"

He coughed and shook his head, and looked down again to his whittling.

I know now how I must have looked at him: from within the well of my being, from within a deep, dark, somehow sacred place where things are born before they take flight to the light.

*

I was overcome by a terrible restlessness. When he was gone, I wondered when he would return; when he returned, he was still not there. I wanted him to talk to me, to say things of great philosophical significance; instead he whittled, or fiddled with his fishing gear, getting ready to go off again. I could not concentrate on my own existence; at the time I thought that it was because I needed him to lighten this dark loneliness, and that he did not need me.

One day he came to me with a wink and the slightly ironic smile he used when he had to be polite.

"Will you cut my hair and trim my beard?"

I laughed. "Silly! What with?"

"The knife should do, it's plenty sharp." To demonstrate, he severed a lock of hair and flipped it over his shoulder.

I looked at him. His hair was nearly to his shoulders, his beard ragged and wild; the light in his eyes was all the brighter, more intense, for so much dark hair.

He handed me the knife. "Please? It's so hot and sticky with all this hair. I feel like an English sheepdog in Khartoum."

"I'll see what I can do."

"You're swell."

We were in the shade by the shelter. He took a battered piece of palm trunk which we used as a stool. I thumbed the knife; he sat before me, expectantly.

I touched his hair, hesitantly at first, lifting the dark, salt-encrusted strands away from his scalp, exploringly. We had no comb, no soap; our hair was layered with oils and salt and inescapable sand, and only a good downpour could give it any semblance of cleanliness. A musky smell rose on my fingers.

"What would the gentleman like?"

He laughed. "I'll settle for a more . . . medieval look. You know, Hamlet or something like that."

"I'll do what I can."

I worked quietly. I needed all my concentration to pull the hair over the knife blade, then shear; the blade seemed dull for the task.

"Your neck's white," I said after some minutes. "You'll get sunburned."

"Ah, but I feel cooler already." He put his fingers to the back of his neck and in so doing brushed my hand. I pulled away, a reflex, a propriety.

"Yes, all you can cut, up to here." He showed me; I put my hand there to confirm. His skin was warm, damp.

When I had finished, his hair was ragged around his neck, but shorter and cooler. I walked around to face him, checking from the front for evenness, avoiding his inquisitive gaze, yet so close, in his periphery, touching his hair. His eyes followed me, a boy's eyes, nervous, apprehensive for his self-image—an image which could, ultimately, only reflect upon me. We were each other's mirrors; we could shine only in each other's eyes.

"Perhaps you could cut mine when I've finished," I suggested. "I hate this long hair."

He nodded. "Careful now," he said, as I approached his beard, "this hurts." His jaw stiffened as I pulled the tender strands away, slice, slice, sometimes yank. He had always cut his beard himself, sometimes with disastrous, bloody results, until he had finally decided to let it grow, to hell with it; but now it was so hot, and he worried about "fleas and critters," he said.

I found that if I proceeded quickly, he could grit his teeth and bear it; the end result was an improvement, neater, closer.

I stood back and looked at him. He smiled, hoping for my approval. In my mind I saw not the clumsy results of a scissorless haircut but the radiance of pleasure that this licensed intimacy had given me. His smell, his skin, the resonance of his laughter beneath my fleeting touch, there, so close to me.

"Your turn now."

I sat on the overturned stump and handed him the knife. I closed my eyes. As I used to do, at the hairdresser's. I waited for the tugging pain, but felt only a soft rubbing: his fingers were massaging my scalp and a shiver went through me, sweet and violent.

"What are you doing?"

"In Port-au-Prince, there was this old woman who cut my hair, Mama Lucie; she always used to massage my scalp before cutting, she said it relaxes the roots."

"You should have said. I would have done it to you."

"Next time. Watch how I do it."

It poured into me from the tips of his fingers, the reverberations of a tingling sensation which ran deep into memory. When I was a child, my sister and I used to play hairdresser's, sometimes for hours; she would brush my hair and bring on this delicious sensation, innocent yet narcotic, and I would demand that she stand there and brush, over and over . . .

When he came to cut my hair I felt no pain. Then he had finished and he fluffed my new curls out over my ears, and I longed to keep his hands there. The hot stickiness at my neck was replaced by coolness. I sat on, dreamy, and let the sensation fade away like ripples on a pond.

"You okay?" he asked.

I opened my eyes and smiled. "Yes, thanks, much cooler."

He looked at me, pleased, serious. At our feet a small pile of clippings, fair and dark, curled together on the sandy ground.

We grew shy with each other. Two children who have discovered too much pleasure in each other's company. We became mutually elusive, our moods like the ever-shifting bolts of light that curtained through the palm trees. We knew this somehow, and it did not worry us. There was a complicity, a shared anticipation.

Sometimes I lay on my back in the shelter with the heat thick upon me and I thought of him lying next to me, just there, an arm's length away, and what it might be like if we could drop our cloak of shyness, if we were to cross over that arm's-length barrier.

Easier to fly three quarters of the way around the world than to cross that short distance.

He slept and snored and snuffled quietly. How could he sleep, with that weight of heat?

At dawn, when the sun was below the spreading roof of palm branches, it would puncture the shelter with small dots of light, like the light through louvered shutters or through the small round skylights in the dome of a Turkish hamam: tender, new-born light, dappling his cheek as he slept.

He usually rose early to go fishing, before the worst heat of the day. Sometimes he fished from the raft with our precious line, from the middle of the lagoon; more often he dived with his spear, quickly, near the shore, keeping a constant watch for sharks. Perhaps their presence added an element of thrill, of real risk, to our otherwise predictable island existence. He was never frightened. When he saw a shark coming, he walked out of the lagoon, casually, as if he had had enough anyway. I usually joined him later in the morning to help clean and prepare the fish for drying; sometimes we cooked it right away. We joked about the varieties of fish as if they represented the whole range of a five-star French restaurant's menu. Delicate, small fish were our veal, our chicken; the meatier ones were our Sunday roasts. Shrimp, crab, and octopus were our appetizers, or even our dessert.

One day I came down to the beach at the lagoon and he was not there. His fishing tackle lay in a small pile near the life raft, in the shade and well out of reach of the tide. I called, looked around me, but there was no answer; I walked to the northern edge of the lagoon, then to the south, but wherever I went I was alone, and my calls went unanswered. I sat for a long time looking out into the lagoon, watching the changing hues of turquoise and aquamarine reflect the passage of clouds overhead. I thought—grim presage—of what it would be like to be utterly alone on the island, and I feared for myself, and for him, and for the future. Black clouds were drawing in from the horizon, growing in intensity with each approaching mile like successive washes of color on a canvas. Was it then that I understood, beneath that threatening sky, how precious his existence must be to me, and mine to him? It was more than mere survival; it was something which lifted me from where I sat and set me running along the western shore, pacing my footfall to the rhythm of the first big drops of rain which now shattered upon the sand. I ran, drenched in my own sweat, then in the chill of the wind-driven downpour, until I found him.

He sat hugging his knees, at the foot of a tree, his eyes focused on some melancholy thought in the middle distance. I stopped short and waited for him to see me; for a moment I did not exist, so strong was the loneliness that surrounded him like an armor. When he looked up, his eyes were not eyes I had ever seen, but pools swelling with the flood of some unspoken sadness. We stared at each other, alarmed, like strangers; then he got to his feet, slowly, as if measuring the irrevocability of a choice. There was a pause, a hesitation as he looked at me, a breathlessness of uncertainty. Then he took a few steps, as I did, to close the distance between us at last with our arms and lips and rain-graced bodies.

*

The words poured from us, meaningless, tender, hurried words, suddenly less important than touch, than the rain upon our closed eyelids.

Where have you been? he murmured. Have you no idea how I've wanted you, damn it, woman, always wandering off with your confounded poetry—

Looking for you, I replied. I lost you, that day the ship—no, it wasn't you I lost, it was the old you, and the old me, it all changed—

You make no sense, yet I understand you, I know what you mean to say—

God, you feel so good—

Did we die and go to heaven?

I've wanted you too, so badly, only I didn't know it—

He tasted of rain and salt and the sea.

*T*hose first days, or weeks, of which there was no counting, were given to each other. Often I lie back and the longing returns, preserved through generations of cells in my body, the tradition of memory passed down unchanged over the years. Still strong. Still desiring. Because of what happened when we were both at the height of desire, looking down at the ordinary, forgetful world.

The memory of skin, open to those fingers, notes forever played in that same music. Skin against skin, sun-warmed, rough like sand or smooth like the waters of the lagoon. Lips, speaking in tongues comprehensible only to the body. Fluids, smells, sounds. My breasts filling and rising to be nearer his touch; his sex in mine and the place we would travel at that moment, a place of homecoming. A moment which transcended the physical, yet justified it. It was always there, both promise and reward, if we listened well; it informed our entire existence yet negated it, being made of pure insubstantial desire, propelling us into oblivion.

Each became the other's willing prisoner; we gave ourselves gladly to the gentle tyranny of the present. Had we but known, could we have loved before, and rescued all those moments which had been lost to despair? Or had despair actually heightened the intensity of this sudden burst of color, like rain before blossoming?

But we did not think of that, then. We were our own world; we became the island as it became our temple. We continued to walk and swim and fish, but it was as if we were newly arrived in this remote tropical paradise, by choice.

T had always been very shy about love, or sex. I never had that many boyfriends, or suitors; I was of two minds about the whole business. First of all, it was the way we were brought up, Pidge and me, good Victorians. Good upright daughters of Kansas. You were taught to defer to your husband, behind closed doors, under heavy counterpanes. But I felt, already as a girl, that I must strive for something else, something better for women, that would free us from the Victorian tutelage of our sex. And, ironically, sex and love seemed to get in the way— because they were at the heart of the problem. So to achieve what I wanted to achieve, a part of me tried to become asexual. Yet I was lauded for my achievements because I was a woman.

With my husband—

No, never mind him; not that he wasn't good to me, but he was merely a stop on my way to discovery, I see that now. A stop behind closed doors, at that. It took a wild windswept island to lead me away from my past, from the old realities, to teach me, to free me. And a man who had sailed the trades and all the oceans, who knew the wind and the exhilaration.

He shocked me at first—his appetite, his lack of inhibition. When I demurred, he would protest: but there's no one here. He teased me, called me prissy, prudish. Which I was. Until I understood the burden of society I still carried; until I saw that he, as a man, had always been free in such matters, free and wild and joyful, whereas I had been rigid and scared and, at best, tolerant. With my husband I had waited on the sidelines while my body got on with it, and merely enjoyed, a bemused spectator. (What a different story ours might have been, if . . . But that is idle speculation.) In the act of love I had not engaged my spirit, had not known it was possible to experience more, to loosen the mind's control and let the body sing, like an animal calling deep in the bush. Until the island, I did not even suspect it was possible to want to open oneself so entirely, to let all one's desire and all one's secret joy flow towards the same place. Upriver, to the source.

He was my boatman, he took me there.

All the past we had buried was brought to light again to enhance and refine our vision of each other. At last we could talk freely, without pain, because the past had acquired a new purpose.

And there was suddenly so much to talk about that there were not enough hours in the day. Long after dark we lay together in the shelter or on our backs under the stars, sleepless in a torrent of words. We did not care that we had no idea what state our poor world was in, we talked as if we had just read the day's paper, arguing about politics and how to solve the world's problems. We both felt we were experts on the matter, having seen so much of the world, more than the average politician, in fact; from our remote atoll we were able to depose dictators and confer democracy and enlightenment on all the beleaguered nations on earth. It seemed that simple.

Our own hearts were more complex. We would talk around our families, then grow hesitant as we approached the center, our respective spouses. We knew that in another world, in our old world, what we were doing was wrong, even cruel, and that if ever we were rescued we would cause much pain.

"But we cannot cause any more pain," he said. "They think we're dead, love, you know that, you know they'll be living their own lives again—"

"But what if they're not? What if at this very moment my husband is stomping down corridors and banging on desks in Washington, seeking support for another rescue attempt—" I imagined, briefly, a great warship steaming towards our island, then I fell against him, and held him. "I couldn't bear for them to part us now. I couldn't bear it."

"They won't," he whispered, his lips against my ear.

*

It was so hot in the middle of the day, but the heat entered our bodies and left us restless with longing. We would go to the lagoon and laugh as the refracted image of our bodies in the water formed a strange sea creature, neither swimming nor floating nor standing, but suspended in the weightless urgency of pleasure.

I envied him his extraordinary life—he was full of stories and adventures. As a young man—when I was still in school, trying to decide my future—he had gone to sea, rounding Cape Horn no less than seven times. He had been shipwrecked; he had saved others from shipwreck and worse. He told a story of French sailors rescued from the ice floes, of a Portuguese fisherman who had been adrift for a month in his dory. There were the cities he had visited, the exotic ports and postings, where he had been free to live his mad, carousing life to the fullest. I had been to those places too, but always in the protection of a local diplomat or dignitary, always at one remove from the real life of the place, from its brothels and dives and rowdy seaside crowds. My life paled in comparison. I told him this.

"But you've done more than any woman has ever dreamed of doing," he protested, as if that could somehow make up for what I hadn't been able to do. "You're to the women's cause what Lindbergh is to aviation."

This was a cruel gibe. I felt a red flush of anger. "No. I wanted to be to aviation . . . what Lindbergh is to aviation."

He raised his eyebrows.

"You've missed the point," I said. "Women have to be judged on their own merit alongside men, not just because they are women."

"And do you think you have been?" he challenged me, his eyebrows still raised above a trace of blue irony.

How little it mattered here, now, where there was no one else to judge; but was he not the most important judge? Did it not matter deeply what he thought?

"No," I said. "Whatever I have done that may equal or better a man's achievement, I have been seen from a different perspective, I know this. So it seems that what matters to people is not the accomplishment but the perception."

"But don't you want to be special? Because as a woman you always will be—"

"I don't need to be, I already am," I said crossly. "Don't you think that what I—we—have done is remarkable?"

He shook his head and shrugged. "No, not really. It was all set up for us—for you; it was a gorgeous stunt."

"Oh, really?"

"Don't get mad now, I'm being truthful. It was special because you're a woman—even the very fact you were able to enlist everyone's cooperation—"

"It wasn't me, it was my—my husband, and you know it. He hired you."

"To his everlasting regret, I suppose."

"Please, let's stop this bitterness, none of it matters now in the least, does it?"

"No, it doesn't," he said softly. "Except that you're still the finest man I've ever met."

I remember his thumb under my chin, his fingers curled against my cheek. Then he said, "And to prove it, you can do the fishing for a change."

I took his spear and ran glad and fearless into the water. I knew my limbs to be strong and brown like any native's. The blue waters closed around me as I dived, a sweet captivity, a tender rediscovery of the world.

"Why were you such a heavy drinker?" I asked him one day.
He sat whittling, cross-legged, in the shade; chips of driftwood

scattered at his feet, on his toes. I watched his hands, jealous of their activity.

"Crazy, I guess. Can't stop myself. If a keg of whiskey"—he rolled his eyes skyward—"washed up on the beach, I wouldn't stop till I'd drunk it all, or passed out first. I'm the all-time drunken sailor."

"But why?"

"I need it. Like I need you."

"But it made you so . . . awful. My mother's life was destroyed by my father's love of alcohol. Don't you care—"

He shrugged. "Can't help it. No, I don't care. It gives me pleasure."

"Would you stop if I asked you? I mean, if ever—"

He looked hard at me, defiantly. He put his knife down and crawled over to me, and then took me by the shoulders. "Careful, now. Would you ask me to choose, you mean?"

I nodded.

He shook his head. "I'm a weak man. Be glad we're on a desert island, and you're my only liquor. Does it matter if I can't get enough of you? Ever? If I'm drunk on you all the time?"

"It doesn't matter," I whispered. "I feel the same way."

$\mathcal{I}$t rained a lot that year and we would stand naked by the shelter and bathe in the warm flood from the full-bellied clouds; bathe and kiss and gulp for each other; touch and smooth and curl our limbs around each other; then laugh, when it was over, at our raisin-shriveled fingertips, like children who have stayed too long in the bath.

If I close my eyes, and lie back, and open my mind to the past, he comes and sits beside me cloaked in a soft dust of lost time, and his brief presence is a tonic of youth.

To age has no single antonym: to youthen? Scientifically, it does not happen. But on our island, it happened, out of time. We grew strong and smooth; the gray disappeared from his beard. The more we laughed, the more the little lines around our eyes faded.

But I speak from retrospect. At the time, it did not matter. Had we been gray and stiff and wrinkled, it would not have made any difference. Each day disregarded time. We had entered other realms, other latitudes.

His sex frightened me, as my own words still frighten me under the stars. We often sat naked in those days, in the shade, in the pleasure we took in each other's body, in our need for immediacy. But I found myself looking furtively at the creature between his legs, examining its rawness, its deceptive tranquillity, and I knew it to be dangerous, because it seemed to have its own compelling existence, quite detached from emotion. It was not like my own sex, which became raw and suffused with emotion and desire because it was inside me, part of me, part of that same compulsion towards the man who had graced my existence. Sometimes I could not forgive him his manhood; I wanted him to be like me in all things.

*

"Do you think," I asked one day, "do you think there ever could have been anything between us—back there?"

He guffawed, and scratched the back of his neck. "No. You weren't my type."

"And now you favor the desert-island type?"

"Now I've got no choice."

His words stung. I stood up from the sand where we sat and walked to the water's edge. A fish jumped in the lagoon. The sun had set, leaving a velvet drape against the evening sky.

But there was truth in what he said. I had no choice; he had not been my type either. He was there of necessity; what I had known of him was that he could navigate, that he would help to further my goal. Of the man I knew little; at the fore was my fear of his drunkenness—the horrible times when it was necessary to *pour* him back onto the plane. I had never seen him, really seen him, and yet he had been there, often not drunk at all, beside me, for weeks. Handing me in and out of the plane, or a car, or a ricksha. Standing behind me for the photographers. Escorting me to my hotel room, or my place at dinner. Helping me up the steps of the temple at Rangoon—although he would not follow me in.

I had not seen him. Had not felt the heartbeat guiding the light pressure of his hand at my elbow, had not known the man behind the firm grasp which helped me aboard the plane. I would never have seen him, back in that other world.

He stood behind me now and his arms went slowly around my waist. "Do you believe," he murmured, "that we are our true selves *here*, or back there?"

"I don't know. So much—"

"So much got in the way of who we are, who we can be. You were an enactment of yourself because you were onstage so much of the time, and I was a shadow of myself . . . in your shadow. Now we are alone, and free of all that—"

"But you're saying any man and woman thrown together on a desert island—"

"Perhaps . . . the man would eventually try to conquer the woman, regardless of their feelings for each other—"

"But that's grotesque!" I turned to face him. I felt tears in my eyes which I could not stop. "Is that it, then? Is that all there is between us, that *eventually* you have conquered me, because of your appetite, because you could no longer stand your *celibacy*—"

"And you? You've been as willing as I have—"

I took a few steps away from him. "Is that all there is then, between two people—circumstances?"

"Was your husband . . . not ideal in your former circumstances?"

I did not answer. I did not ask him about his wife. I stooped to pick up a shell that had washed in at my feet like a message; when I rose, he stood by me and took my hand.

"Come," he said. "Let me tell you a story about desire and circumstances. About what would have been right, if I had been older and wiser and had listened to my soul. Because circumstances created a chance to seize the beauty of the moment, just as we have done. A chance to see our true selves revealed—not just someone's ideas of 'types' from society."

"So you don't think any two people—"

"No, not at all. You know yourself, if either of us was with our real spouse here, it would not be the same."

"It would not be paradise." I handed him the shell.

"No, not paradise."

"Tell me your story."

"One year I signed on one of the last clipper ships to round the Horn. Just before they opened the Canal. We were northward-bound again, for New York; we'd had nothing but gales and sickness on board for weeks. Christ Jesus, what a place that is; I don't know if there's any territory you could fly over anywhere in the world to compare with a passage by ship round the Horn. Cold, wet, constantly on the edge of existence—like flying on one bad engine over tropical rain forest, maybe that's what it's like, with nowhere to land. Only at sea it goes on for weeks.

"We called at Port Stanley to drop off some supplies to those poor islanders. And a godforsaken place that is, too, even after the Horn—you know how bad some people must have had it back in England to want to emigrate to the goddamn South Atlantic.

"We were ready to leave again as soon as we could, but a series of gales kept us in port. One of those things in life, you think afterward that there was a reason for it. Like us being here, after all.

"It didn't take long to visit what was there. The town was lonely; there was a sort of small public hall where they held dances on a Saturday, but you'd go along and all you'd see was dour farmers and their prim pale wives and a few young kids; if there were any young women in that place, they must have been under lock and key.

"We were sitting there one night, me and my friend Joey, from Chicago like me, and we were missing the city, talking about all the things we'd do when we got home, when this woman walked in, alone, and the room went sort of quiet—just a hush for people to look up and see who it was, but Joey and I stopped and had a good look because she was alone. Not pretty or anything, plain and thin and more sunburned than was usual for women in those days; a sharp, red nose on her, overworked-looking. But she had one of those smiles that are like a waif in the cold knocking on the door to be let in, and eventually one of the farmers called out to her—Jane her name was, see what I mean, plain—and she went and sat with them.

"Joey and I watched the dancing for a while, then went back on to the ship, not even drunk or anything. The next day I went ashore on my own to go for a walk. I tried to find a packet of smokes, but it was Sunday and they were all at church, so I started up through the town. No one in the streets—a few dogs, a stray sheep. I got a mile or two outside the town when I saw a cottage with smoke coming out of the chimney. It looked such a warm sight, I thought I'd knock and see if I could buy any breakfast or fresh eggs, just for something to do—not that they'd take my dollars.

"It was the woman from the dancing. She looked at me, not afraid, almost as if she'd been expecting me, and said, 'You're from the American ship.' She had a nice accent, real educated, English; she invited me in, I didn't even have time to explain why I'd come and she was putting the kettle on, the whole tea routine, even though it was the wrong time of day.

"I reckon she was the age we are now, maybe a bit more. I wasn't even dry behind the ears, but I took myself for one of those Errol Flynn–type heroes. She didn't seem to mind, she asked me about my travels as if she was anything but old enough to be my mother; she let me talk and boast through tea and cookies and cakes until finally I asked her, when I'd run out of adventures, what she was doing out there.

" 'I came out with my husband, of course,' she said. 'He died, about ten years ago. I'm keeping the farm going. For his sake.'

"I thought about this and couldn't understand why she would bury herself alive there. With the brashness of being young or a Yank or both, I said, why didn't she remarry or sell the farm and move back to England?

"She gave me that smile I'd seen the night before and shook her head; she'd had offers—for the farm, for her hand in marriage —but she'd turned them all down.

"Then she surprised me. 'Would you like to stay? I could use a strong lad like you about the place—I can pay you quite well.'

"I made some sort of coughing noise and shook my head— I had to get back home, I told her, and looked away.

" 'Sweetheart?' she asked, almost coyly; I shook my head, I was embarrassed, but there was some truth in it, there were a few girls I was sweet on. But when I looked at her she had her eyes down like she was counting the crumbs in her lap.

" 'I'd better go,' I said. 'Thank you for the tea.' She stood up as if to walk me to the door, but when I got there she had her back against the door and a frightened look on her face.

" 'Please stay for a little while—please, it's early, it's so nice to see a new face—come and play chess with me.'

"I didn't really want to stay but I couldn't think of an excuse, and she'd been kind and interested and I didn't want to hurt her feelings, so I followed her over to a small table by the window which looked out onto the farm, and I looked out—it was so bleak and lonely, like the edge of the known earth.

"We played chess but mostly we talked. I didn't especially like to look at her—there was something in her eyes, as if she could see right into you; her mouth was tight, except when she smiled; but when she talked she made me feel older and important. The Falklanders didn't like her, she said; they spread rumors that she went with men from the ships, or that she had a lover in Argentina. 'What bosh!' She laughed, quietly. 'Do I look the type? I run my farm, I have a small garden, one or two friends in town who are kind to me, and a good library. What do I need with sailors and gauchos?'

"She was a woman after your own heart. She was proud to be running that farm and just because she was a woman alone she was always being criticized by the local people. Maybe she thought that because I was young and a stranger I wouldn't criticize her. I didn't. Besides, in my trade in those days you did sometimes meet strong, unconventional women. Still do.

"But I couldn't figure it out—why she'd bury herself in that place for the rest of her life, when she could sell the farm, go back to England and remarry and be with her own kind. I told her this.

" 'But women don't have their own kind,' she protested gently.

'Whether I'm here or back in England, the constraints are the same—perhaps greater, even. I have a kind of freedom here. Really, people talk, but they leave me alone. They'd never chase me away or hurt me, they have too much respect for my husband's memory. He was a good man.'

" 'And the others?'

" 'What others?'

" 'I mean, the ones who wanted to marry you. After.'

" 'All greedy drunkards; they're after the farm because everything's in place, no hard work to get started. They're not interested in me,' she scoffed.

" 'Are you sure?'

"I don't know why I questioned her like this; maybe I was just trying to make her feel better by getting her to talk about herself. She shrugged and picked up one of the chess pieces and held it against her throat; I could, then, imagine her loneliness, in the way she could squeeze that chess piece against her throat but never hold a warm person in her arms; but then she had her pride, her high standards. Or perhaps it was true about the sailors, the gauchos.

"We abandoned the game and sat there in a nervous silence. Wind rattled the windows; she rose and went to the grate to start a fire. I watched her as she bent over the wood—the elegant curve of her waist, or of her ankle as her skirt lifted away from the floor. I felt stupid, yet I suddenly wanted her. Just then. Just as she bent to light the fire, after all the sad, true things she'd said, not before. Until then I'd had an idea of what she was, what she must be; I'd only seen how plain she was, and I'd only seen her as others, no doubt, must see her.

"Maybe it was different for her with me; maybe she was just starved and lonely, and I was young and ready to grasp life like a schooner with the wind in her sails. I knew how to listen to her and let her be. Maybe that was enough.

"She came to me after she'd built the fire; she took my hand and led me away into her bedroom, without saying a word. The bed had a white crocheted counterpane; she folded it and laid it on the chair, neatly, carefully; then she did the same with her clothes and mine.

"I nearly missed the ship. I nearly stayed to work for her. I regret to this day that I didn't."

He didn't speak for a moment, his gaze fixed upon a point in the distance where neither of us could go. Then he looked down, and murmured, "My point is, she was lonely, she could have had all the men she wanted, whatever she may have said. But she didn't. She waited, with me, until she thought she wanted me, could trust me. And I could have seen her as the others did—easy prey, a lonely woman—because she was there, and circumstances made it easy. No. All circumstances had done was to place her in my path. I know I was young, too young, maybe, but I sensed something about her. I would have loved her, if I had stayed.

"I guess—I guess before it was clear to me how you felt, I would sit watching you and remember her, all those years ago. As if our time here was—is—precious. As if there's a ship waiting somewhere, after all—for one of us."

He paused for a moment, not looking at me. Then he continued, so quietly I could hardly hear him.

"When I called at Port Stanley a year or so later, the house was closed, shuttered. I asked at the tobacconist's . . . they told me she'd died."

"A sickness?"

He shook his head. "In childbirth."

"Had she married, then, after all?"

"No."

"And the child?"

He didn't answer. He looked at me, sadly, intently, then his eyes dropped to the shell which he still held in his hand, as if he could see into the deep curve of its pink heart. As if some explanation might lie hidden there for what had happened so long ago.

$\mathcal{W}$e gave up talk of our desert-island desire and let our feelings rule. We loved, yet did not speak the word, for fear: its weight, its finality. We did not need it; perhaps the word was some residual notion from civilization, created to encompass and define. We were defined by the island alone, and by the presence of the other. To name would have meant to enclose, and we were learning a new freedom.

He made combs from the fine gray pieces of driftwood. We would sit in the shade and comb each other's hair, a ritual, honoring that first time. Our rituals were not planned; they evolved from a natural order of things, bringing pleasure to the once-long days. There were meals. Fishing. Brief, shark-wary swims into the coral world of the lagoon. Gathering of wood for the fire, which had to be carefully maintained. Repair and maintenance of the shelter. Gathering of coconuts and taro root. Combing the shore for what the ocean did not need that might be precious to us. Bathing at the spring. Talking, usually at sundown: memories and tales, sharing what we had within. Times, too, for solitary meditation, which gave our reunion renewed intensity. And sleep, the only time we might be apart in spirit, though we often slept with hands joined.

Only our lovemaking defied ritual, to mirror the spontaneity of the winter rains. Shows of light, sudden violence, gentle nourishment.

We were lying on the beach by the lagoon. It had rained and the newly returned warmth of the sun added to the joy of his hands upon me. And his skin, smooth and fresh beneath my fingers, beneath my lips, salt and sun-baked.

"Are you jealous?" he said suddenly.

"Jealous, me? Of whom? How can I be jealous if there's no one here?"

"No, I didn't mean now. I mean in general . . . or in the past."

"Why do you ask? The past cannot reach us here."

He was silent, then said, "But it can."

"Tell me."

"Sometimes . . . sometimes I think if it hadn't been *me*, if Manning had stayed on the flight and not quit after the crash in Honolulu—"

"That Manning would be here now?"

He nodded.

"That I would be holding his hand against my lips to bite the salt from his fingers?"

"Don't."

"Well, don't you be silly. Your reasoning is absurd. How can you be jealous of a hypothetical situation? If he were here, you'd be with your wife."

"But there have been so many men in your life. I am jealous. Take Mantz—"

"Don't be ridiculous! Professional, all professional! Your women were not—"

"But what I mean to say is . . . sometimes I wonder if you love me because I'm here. I'm the only one here. Adam and Eve."

"And I can say the same to you, you wonderful fool . . . Have you forgotten what you told me the other day? I thought we'd been through this, I thought we agreed that it wasn't just circumstances, that if you were here with your wife and I with my husband we could not feel this way, even with them . . . I know what I feel with you, I know the freedom and happiness you give me, I know you are all things to me. That I might never have known you otherwise . . . Don't spoil it."

His gaze darkened and grew troubled. Then he buried his head against my neck like a child, and began to sob, to grasp me tighter, trying to pull me into his sorrow.

"I know this. Of course I know this. But I need you," he whispered. "It frightens me, this solitude . . . If you're not there, no one's there. I need to know that it's me that you see, that you want. If you don't see me, I don't exist."

"Oh, silly man . . . I see you, I want you. You've given me back my whole existence, just by being who you are."

But as I said those words and we silenced his sorrow with touching, I knew that was not quite true. The island, too, had begun to give me back my existence, and he was but a part of that greater, sharper universe.

Always, hidden and dangerous like the reef beyond the lagoon, there lay the fear of change or loss, the threat of solitude. I do not know if he felt it as strongly as I did—perhaps mine was a woman's fear, men being by nature more sanguine about such fears—but I worried, and thought of accident or disease and the ensuing terror of loss. He did not know it—for his intent had been different—but his story of the Falkland Islands remained with me as an illustration not of love but of loss. Nor did he see my anxiety each time he cut himself, which was often, as he fished in coral or whittled his combs and trinkets.

But then one day he said, "I think we should get married."

He was whittling; we were in the shelter, for the sky was gray and wind-streaked. I laughed, then I saw that he was serious.

"What do you mean, then?" I asked. "How can we get married? I mean, do we need to?"

He put down his wood and his knife and looked at me. "We need to because it's the right thing to do. If we were at home, we would; and if there are spirits on this island they will have their own reasons. I know it can only be symbolic—"

"You mean a ceremony?"

He wiped his mustache with his finger, then shrugged. "You know, something at dawn or sunset or under the stars, some moment, some significant occasion."

"But I feel married to you already, in the best possible way; why should we change what is already perfect?"

He was quiet, as if the question had arisen in spite of him, in response to some deep, disturbing necessity; perhaps the same unspoken fear which haunted me.

I said yes.

We were married at the rising of the full moon, one year, two months and some days after our arrival on the island. We did not speak; we exchanged rings woven from coconut fiber, then kissed. The stars fading moon-blinded at the horizon were our only witnesses.

I cannot say I felt different for being married to him. Our life did not change, I did not suddenly become subservient to my "husband"—not that I ever would have anyway, never had and never would. But there was a change nevertheless, an easing of passion. He called me "wife," therefore I called him "husband." Something from outside, from our former lives, had come into the island, like some colonial power to usurp our native urges and dictates. We loved less often, wandered off without explanation, and stayed away longer; we expected certain things to happen (dinner, work on the shelter) and chided each other when they did not.

Perhaps it was merely the work of time, after all. Time, following us to our remote island, setting up the outposts of habit. I would like to think so. For his sake. I believe our "marriage" meant a great deal to him.

Some weeks later I began to notice another change: my body was no longer in harmony with the circling universe. I could not confirm it for a long time, as I was very lax with the calendar, but this uncalculated liberation from what had always been, to me, one of the most confining aspects of womanhood (even used as an unwritten excuse not to hire women pilots) came as both a blessing and a puzzle. I was not too young for the change of life; nor was I yet too old to have a child.

The idea of the former was not unpleasant—it was so awkward on the island, with such shameful, makeshift remedies. But the idea that I might be pregnant—something which, madly, mindlessly, we had never considered or guarded against—kept me awake until the small hours of the morning in restless agitation, or took me away into dreaming bouts of glaze-eyed absence. Finally Fred would ask, what's wrong? and I would shake my head, evasive and apologetic.

It was madness. With my husband I had never known this fear; I was terrified. It was all bad enough, back there, with the humiliating visits to doctors and hospitals, as if one were an illness to be isolated and sanitized (I'd heard enough from my sister); but here—what sort of chance would either of us have?

I spent days of agonizing indecision. I knew that I would have to tell him, I knew that something must be decided. There might be a way I could provoke a miscarriage—jumping out of trees, eating strange herbs; I never stopped to think of the risk to myself, as I judged childbirth to be a greater risk in any case. I lost touch with the island, as if it were in some way responsible for my predicament. I spent hours in the shelter, weak and lethargic. If Fred suspected anything, he did not show it, perhaps from a desire not to know, or to delay knowledge. He agreed with me that the air was close, sweltering with equatorial summer; outside the shelter we were plagued with mosquitoes and other insects. He left me in peace and went off to fish; I slept, often feverishly, visited by bright, disturbing dreams.

One day I ventured out, determined to try jumping from a palm tree. I felt foolish, childish, lacking the courage to fall from a great-enough height for a really jarring landing. It was a strange children's game, the climbing more strenuous than the landing in the soft sand. After ten minutes of this game I walked to the surf's edge and collapsed in the sand, allowing the tepid waves to wash over my tired limbs. I watched the wind on the whitecaps and with sudden astonishment I knew what it meant to have this child in me, that this child was the fruit both of our love and of the island, and was coming as a gift, not a burden. Had I done irreparable damage with my silly jumping? I regretted my foolishness; I curled up on the sand in an effort to apologize, to comfort, to protect. I imagined the native women of the other islands; they must have children in the most primitive conditions, yet they have them; we had at least fresh water and fire and a certain amount of hygiene. The child became possible. We could let Nature look after us.

I left my fear behind and went to find the child's father.

In the beginning he was upset—such a risk, such a responsibility—but then he held me and kissed me and whispered, "No, no, I'm happy, this is wonderful."

He began to dote on me and spoil me, doing all the fishing, stopping me from running or climbing for coconuts. He gave me double portions of fish and coconut water.

It was a time of great dreaming. Of naïveté and innocence and imagination, a return of childhood make-believe and fairy stories. We played house; we were able to create wonderful stories, drawing on all the unnamed spirits of the island. There would be fairies for our child; we were Wendy and Peter Pan.

We did not hear the ticking of the clock.

One night we could not sleep for the heat and he turned to me and fanned me gently with a fan he had made. He said, almost a whisper, almost as if he didn't intend for me to hear him, "You've got to be all right, little mama, you and the baby."

I laughed softly. "What do you mean?"

"I don't want anything to happen to you. I couldn't bear it."

"Silly. Nothing will happen to us." I looked away, falsely confident; I looked away because I could not accept that he had looked at me with the questioning eyes of someone who is leaving on a long, lonely journey.

He wanted to build a cradle, he said. He began by making a miniature one, planning a framework to be covered with woven leaves, like the shelter. "More a basket than a cradle," he explained, excited and apologetic in the same breath, "a Moses basket. But we'll be able to hang it up and rock it, and it will be more comfortable for the baby."

He set off to hunt for good pieces of wood and returned much later with his arms full of driftwood, leaves, scrub, anything that could be woven into his creation. He whistled and hummed as he worked, and I watched in happy expectancy.

It had been hard to live in the wilderness without a goal, without a future. Now, at last, we had one.

One evening (was it that same evening, or days, weeks later?) we were by the fire and I was grilling some fish from the day's catch. He was very quiet, but we sat peacefully and listened to the night noises, savoring the breeze upon our sun-tired skin. I passed him his plate of fish; he picked at it, nibbled, then put the plate down again.

"What's wrong?" I asked.

"I'm not hungry."

"Is anything bothering you?"

"No, I just feel tired. Too much sun. Too much walking around, for the cradle."

"Yes, you've overdone it. Perhaps you've got a mild case of sunstroke."

"Yes, I suppose that's it."

"Do you want to lie down?"

He shook his head. "I'll wait for you."

In the night I awoke and he was not there next to me. I crawled out of the shelter and called, but he did not answer; I ran to the lagoon, where he sometimes went at night when it was too hot in the shelter. I found him on the beach. He was wet and shivering.

"Go away," he said when he saw me.

"You're sick! Why did you come here?"

"I was so hot, I had to cool off, but now—"

I touched him, tried to lift him from where he lay; his arms were burning. He rose slowly to his knees, I pulled him to his feet and we turned towards the shelter, one hesitant step after another. His burning weight against my side grew heavier and heavier. He seemed to trip, then stumbled to the ground, pulling me down with him.

"The baby," he cried, "the baby—"

"I'm all right, don't worry," I said, and held his head in my lap. "But what about you?"

"I'll be all right . . . feels like I'm drunk, thought I was going to pass out there, am I drunk? Was it that damned coconut water, did it ferment at last?"

"Silly . . . you're sick, you've got to rest. I've got to get you back to the shelter, you've got to have water, sleep . . ."

"If I were drunk I'd be better in the morning, wouldn't I? Wife, will I be better in the morning?"

"Of course you will."

But he was not better in the morning. He lay shivering and burning in turns, his body a brick of heat. He had to crawl off into the bushes at times to be alone in his sickness. I fed him coconut water and a thin cold porridge made from the taro root; it was all

I had. He could hardly swallow; droplets from the porridge clung to his beard. I watched him crawl away and refuse my help and my heart seemed to swell with an unfamiliar pain, hard yet tender to the touch, like breasts, like the baby, love now singed with pity and helplessness.

How many days and nights did I stay with him in the shelter, holding his hand, wiping his brow? There is no record of that time, only regret for hope forever lost. I waited for the fever to break, for the drops of sweat to appear welcome on his brow, but he burned and burned before my eyes, consumed, his flesh wasting away until the skin lay dry against his bones. Two hollow pools of darkness formed beneath his eyes.

Mostly he slept but sometimes we spoke, of the baby, of the island. He was very concerned about the cradle, that he might not finish it in time. Often he seemed to forget where he was, and sometimes looked at me as if he did not know me, muttering to himself and staring at the low ceiling with eyes white and watery with terror.

Then one day he was better, and the fire in his body was gone. The unnatural brightness of his eyes remained, and he was very weak, but he could sit up again. He fixed me with those very bright eyes and said, "Let me look at you."

I smiled. "You're better. Can you eat?"

"I'd eat you if I could, so I guess I can't."

"Some vegetable broth, then?"

"No, let me look at you, no, not like that, without your clothes."

I laughed and obliged him and sat with a sheepish smile on my face, so happy to know that he was better, playing silly games.

He lay down again and closed his eyes, muttering, "Good, that was sweet." He slept for most of the afternoon.

I bathed him that evening, an old piece of flannel shirt soaked in the fresh water of the spring. Over and over, gently wiping his weak, tired body, trying to rub the sickness away, to rub in a clean, new body. If only it were that easy. He lay with his eyes closed and a half-smile on his face. He did not move or talk, but let me bathe him.

When I had finished I sat for a long time stroking his hair back from his forehead. I leaned over to kiss him. His lips were hot and dry and tasted of overripe peach; he barely moved. Then he said, "What time was that appointment in Oakland?"

"What?"

"If we want to get back to Yuma in time to be married before the flight, we'd better hit the road."

I sat back on my heels. His eyes were still half-closed, his expression tired and vacant after days of illness, but his voice was determined and lucid.

I called to him, gently. "Wake up, darling, you're dreaming."

He laughed. "I wish I were. Here I have to go and leave a swell woman behind so I can fly around the world with that famous lady pilot who disapproves of my drinking."

"What are you saying? Wake up, darling, please!"

"I'll miss you, sweetheart, you know that . . . I feel like a soldier going to war. One more for the road, won't you? Come on?"

I handed him a bowl of water; he propped himself on his elbows and drank, then looked up at me in disgust.

"What is this stuff?"

I could not answer.

"Wait a minute," he continued. "What is this, Prohibition again? Can't you give me a drink?"

I burst into tears.

"Is that all you can do, sit there and cry?"

It grew dark in the shelter. In stubborn silence I waited for him to sleep. He would sleep, then be better, no more hallucinations. I washed his brow—the fever had returned, but was not as strong as it had been. He was confused, I told myself, and that was normal; he was so weak and disoriented.

When he slept and his breathing was even, I went for a walk. The night was still and very beautiful. I felt I could reach for the sky and pull down a cluster of stars. So close and clear, like flowers to be gathered, still dew-sparkling, into a basket: Deneb, Arcturus, Capella. Small night beasts scrambled in the brush before my footsteps. Perhaps I prayed. I had prayed so much in those last days—prayed and begged and bargained.

Make him better, O Lord, and you can have the baby. Just make him better.

What terrible things we will say or think. I sit here now by the ever-same lagoon, and the stars are just as close and sharp and I'll never be able to reach them or change what happened or what happens now. Can any of us, ever? Do we only think we can make deals with the Almighty when, in fact, we cannot, because there is no Almighty? Does he not exist only in our imagination to trick us into thinking we have some control, through prayer and devotion—some choice, some chance at redemption?

The stars are hard and bright and immovable, fragments of shattered destinies.

The walk tired me; I went back to the shelter. His breathing was rough, but even. He was hot, but towards dawn he reached for the water, and after he had drunk some of it he reached for me, and kissed me, and held me for a moment before falling away again on the mat.

I slept then, deeply—oh, too deeply! A troubled sleep full of dreams, nightmares of planes falling from the sky, planes full of fish. All the fish drowned when they landed in the lagoon.

When I woke the sun was bright and hot through the chinks in the woven palm leaves of the shelter.

He was not there.

*

I ran to the lagoon; he was not there. I ran to the north of the island, to the south, calling, tracing mad winding circles over the island. I collapsed in exhaustion and despair; there was no answer to my calls.

At that time of year a very strong current sets easterly through the equatorial Pacific. So many things then wash into the lagoon and onto the beach. That year there were dead fish, driftwood, even the stinking carcass of a dolphin. We had joked about the dolphin at the time, but I hadn't wanted to see it as an omen.

That day there was an old tea chest, all the way from China . . .

(I am so weary with the telling of this story. It grows light; it hurts so much to tell it, my voice fails me, yet the story is not quite finished. What is this talk now but an old woman's prattling about tea chests and easterly currents?)

But currents, that's the whole point, you see—where they take us, or where we expect them to be. That morning when he vanished from the shelter I did not go first to the eastern shore because at that time of year nothing washed up there—

Something, in the end, turned my tired feet to the east and I went to the cove where we had arrived, the two of us, so long ago—

I looked out to where we had come from, to the place where I could still see passing ships and sinking airplanes, and in the altered light of late afternoon I thought I could see—close enough for sight but too far for words or hope or love—a small craft, round and rubber of the kind used for life rafts, headed east, in the current.

I was sorry that I had never actually told him I loved him, never said the word. That he had left without the ballast of knowing to steady his course. I would bear my silence like a guilt, forever; it was like leaving a dear friend in an argument, then learning that he has been killed in an awful wreck.

I will never know if he left because he was truly mad, delirious; or because he knew he was going to die and wanted to spare me somehow.

Is that what is called an ultimate sacrifice of love?

But if he had lived?

Perhaps God made a deal, after all.

I must not think of these things. It is late and I am tired. There is no lightening of the burden—even when one unloads the words, all the words, even after all these years. They always return and beg to be spoken, and they rankle inside my head and wring my heart until I must speak.

Sometimes I go to the cove and cry my love and pain. Perhaps he can hear me, somehow.

I would like to think so.

How could I have known, in that happier time, the urgency of voicing my love?

That word, that one little word, had all the power to lighten the load.

*I*t is nearly dark and Lucy has not returned from the island. Robin was angry when she left—childish tantrums over a pot of jam. Over so much more, though, unsaid and inexpressible. Now he feels a grudging, defeated urge to compromise, to make things right again. He pauses in his engine work to switch on the anchor light to guide her back from shore.

On deck all is still and calm. The moon has not yet risen; a few early stars puncture the cobalt dome of the sky. The lagoon lies motionless, a swath of silk against the rougher texture of ocean. Gentle night noises murmur against the surf's pounding on the reef, it too less violent tonight, almost benign.

Robin breathes in the night, the warm air with its fragrance of lingering sunshine. Where has he been, he wonders, all this time, to have been so indifferent to the island's beauty, to his own place therein—worrying about engines, about ghosts? Arguing with Lucy about trivial things. Their sojourn in the island's lagoon has been a sojourn out of this world, out of the known world. It has been a journey through a looking glass, where they could have taken the chance to see themselves in their true, hidden, reflection—as they really are, not as they claim to be. And they have failed to see, caught up as they are in their petty disputes, their celestial worksheets and engine manuals and their demand to know the facts.

He goes below to tidy away his tools. He is satisfied; the engine is nearly finished, this time. One last adjustment, he is confident, will solve the problem. To savor his progress, his hopefulness, he will leave this last job until morning. He takes a warm beer from the locker and returns to the deck. He sits out on the bowsprit, closer to the lagoon, to the island. Water laps against the hull; the boat rocks gently.

The beer is bitter and too warm, but it intensifies his thoughts and dramatizes them. I must share this night with Lucy, he thinks; I must apologize, take her in my arms, tell her how wrong we have been to give in to tension, to let it rule us. As if by not rebelling against it we could delude ourselves. As if we could continue to live like the people in shiny yachting magazines, smiling and flat and perfect under a cloudless tropical sky; closed, false, entrapped by pride.

He finishes his beer and watches the shore, knowing she will come soon, resigned and, perhaps, apologetic. They will hold each other and kiss; each will say, "It's my fault," and fault, at least, will evaporate on the waves of their laughter, seaward.

He will surprise her. He jumps up and goes below to prepare dinner. He hurries, because he knows she will be here soon. It is late already; she may even be a bit frightened by the darkness.

Candles. A rare tin of pâté; some olives, pickled peppers, a potato salad. Bread and crackers. They must reach port soon, he thinks; they are nearly out of yeast. Wineglasses rubbed until they sparkle. Robin surveys his work proudly, filled with the rare pleasure of loving domesticity.

The moon has risen. He can just make out the dull form of the rubber dinghy on the beach—where is she? What can be keeping her?

A composite of all the vicious gap-toothed pirates or cannibals Melville or Stevenson could have imagined irrupts in the tranquillity of the night. All sarcastic, evil laughter; all dread and horror.

As night lengthens, so does Robin's conviction that he must find the ghost, person, islander, whatever, whoever it is; he must return to the island at first light and search, really search. There must be someone there. There have been too many unexplained occurrences out of the realm of everyday absentmindedness or eccentricity.

The paperback; the almanac; the jam; the radio; the disappearing dinghy; the bowl of coconut water. And the fresh water, of course, in their own water tanks. So there must be a spring somewhere, and the ghost is a helpful one, a sharing one.

This too seems impossible, ridiculous. There is no one on the island—no one could survive on that piece of parchment. They would have come when *Stowaway* first arrived to beg for passage to Tarawa.

But even Robin knows that not everything or everyone need conform to his brittle Western logic: natives will have their own way—their own religion, customs, superstitions.

He will search, tomorrow.

Meanwhile, the pâté goes brown; where is Lucy?

Perhaps she is angry, so angry that she is staying away to spite him, to call forth his anxiety and worry him into appreciating her. If that is the case, then it is a cruel game. He hesitates to swim ashore, then admits to his own cowardice. Perhaps he should not tempt fate.

Resigned, fighting surges of bitterness, Robin puts the dinner things away. Too restless to sleep, he returns to his engine. They must get out of there—something is destroying them.

Robin dreams. He has fallen asleep over the engine.

In his dream he is loving. It is not Lucy, but a faceless woman whom he desires, who is everything to him, more important than life itself. He has never known such happiness—yet he knows, too, that he is dreaming. He tries to see her face; he needs to see her face to know that this is not a dream. But she eludes him, turning away, revealing to Robin only the porcelain smoothness of her body. He pleads and reaches out to touch her, she must not escape him, his survival somehow depends upon her. Her warmth burns him; he awakes.

His hand is on his work lamp. It is three o'clock in the morning. Lucy is not there.

He stares through darkness at the moonlit island. What is it that disturbs him so about the place—is it the wild unpredictability of its virgin nature, or rather what is *not* there? No inhabitants, no police station, no infrastructure of society and humanity. It is outside the sphere of his experience, outside knowledge or control. Its primeval beauty is insolent, and says to him, I don't want you, I don't need you. There is no place for you here.

What does Lucy find there—despite her fear of the footprint? She too has spoken of the island's hostility—yet she is not afraid to spend a night there. As if she prefers, at this moment in her life, the island. Are women better able to commune with the spirit of place?

Memories shine, crystallized in brightness. Lucy, as he saw her one day in the school library, bent over a volume of Matthew Arnold—the slight, bemused tilt of her head which aroused so gently in Robin the realization that he was falling in love with her. The cliffs by Tintagel, where they stood and shouted happy nonsense into the deaf escaping wind, and her cheeks flushed with the bloom of springtime against the gray gray sky; they had hugged and danced like two children in that place; among all, most haunted by the fairies and spirits of the imagination. Your Guinevere to my Lancelot, he had said then; now he has become Arthur, wondering at lost worlds.

We are no longer those two cliff-happy lovers, he thinks; of course we have changed, of course life changes. But to retrieve the joy of that moment, if not of an era, to retrieve the capacity to love—is that so impossible?

How have I lost her? he asks in the early hours, his head against the mast, his eyes to the stars. Because I have lost her, she is not happy with me anymore, not really, only now and again when we have to forget ourselves, just to keep going . . . Is it just the trip which is too hard on her, on us, or is there something more permanent, deep-seated, that cannot be moved or changed? We're like two strangers here; I don't know what she thinks, or wants; she only speaks to complain or project things; nothing is reality. Everything which should have been so simple has become so complicated.

The boat creaks, the anchor chain groans quietly. Shall I, must I, let her go, if it comes to that? Can I carry on alone? The boat understands me, the boat responds: it is a possibility.

Dawn at last. The horizon has never seemed farther, or lonelier.

*D*aybreak rouses Lucy from her dream-filled bed of sand. She sits up, confused; the sky is gray and mournful. Not a tropical sky but a sky from the north, ominous, implacable. There is no wind.

She shakes her head to rid herself of sand and sleep; she did not mean to spend the night here. Robin will be desperate with worry, she thinks, then remembers their argument and wants to say, Well, good. He deserves to worry. But her long sleep and the cold hours of dawn have numbed and softened her, throwing this new gray light upon the memory of yesterday's heat.

She turns to get up and by her hand is a crude brown bowl, the half of a coconut shell, filled with a pale liquid. She hesitates, recalling Robin's fury, but she knows no such anger, no reason to refuse this simple gift. She drinks and while drinking thinks of her strange night on the sand, wondering that she never woke in fright, neither cold nor lonely, as if drugged by sleep and dreams.

She has dreamed and her dreams slip from her as she swallows; her spirit remains full of sadness and loss. She rises and walks along the eastern shore for a time, looking, waiting for the sun, but it remains behind a wall of gray. There is no knowing if it has, indeed, already risen. There is no cheer to this daylight, only a heavy, inexplicable loneliness.

She cannot see the boat from where she walks. Her solitude is complete. On other days, when she came to walk and meditate, she was equally alone, but the sun's rays seemed to light her future with warmth and presence. Now her sense of isolation is washed with the bleakness of the blocked gray horizon. What must it be like to be stranded in such a place, to be utterly alone and friendless? Her arguments with Robin begin to seem trivial and pointless when held up against such solitude.

She turns her steps to the west, with an involuntary shiver.

*

Robin greets her with reproach, concern laced with anger. She climbs up from the dinghy and looks into his half-angry, half-loving face. He helps her aboard; she puts her hands behind his neck to pull him closer. She kisses him, chastely, then says, "I'm sorry. I fell asleep."

"All night? How could you stay all night?"

"I was tired, I suppose . . . It was peaceful there."

"I was sick with worry! I thought the island's ghost had got you. I haven't slept—"

She did not expect so many protestations. She thought her safe return would suffice; but then she also expected the sun to come out today. Her smile turns rueful; he is looking at her with bewilderment. She must not tell him about the coconut water.

"I'm sorry," she repeats, "I don't know . . . such strange dreams." She shakes her head, as if to clear it of any remaining sleep, to clear herself for him.

He shrugs, then smiles, pleased with what he is about to tell her. "I fixed the engine during the night," he beams, waving the key at her.

"Really! How?"

"I don't know . . . inspiration of a kind; I just tried something different." He dangles the engine key in front of her, elated. "It worked, finally, just before dawn. Didn't you hear me?"

"No . . . perhaps I was too far away. Does that mean we can leave soon?"

"Soon, soon. Just a bit of fine-tuning, stow things away. Though I don't like the look of these clouds."

"Neither do I—"

"Perhaps we should wait for a day."

She agrees; her relief is immense. When the sky clears they will leave and be free from the strange spirits of the place.

*

She goes below and makes coffee. Its rich, pungent smell suffices to comfort, to restore the certainty of belonging, of having a place on earth. She pictures fields of workers picking the green raw beans; then dusty tropical towns where great burlap sacks lie piled in the sun. Teeming humanity, communing through cups of coffee; a human chain, like a food chain. Linked. She laughs.

Robin cannot hear her, he is on deck preparing the boat for departure. His steps resound overhead, purposeful. He must be pleased, she thinks, he has fixed his engine and I have returned, compliant. There has been no further talk of looking for the ghost.

Her smile fades when, with the first swallow, the coffee rises in her throat, unwelcome, nauseating. She is reminded of what she has tried so hard to ignore, or disprove by an effort of will: that she must be pregnant. She will have to tell Robin, and see what they can agree upon. She wants to return to Honolulu, by air, if necessary, for an abortion. He must see they cannot continue the cruise if she is pregnant.

But will he accept her terms?

She cannot see the sky, but it has come through the opened hatch and porthole to weigh upon her with its bleakness.

Robin pauses for a moment to look towards the island. The palm trees droop in the still air against the dark slate of the sky. He feels a storm in the windless weight of air and looks for a moment at the spare anchor; no, he thinks, it's just nervousness, setting a second anchor is such a bother, and we have the engine now. There is no wind, no danger. There will be ample time to set the second anchor if the wind does pick up.

Somewhere on that island there is someone: no ghost, he is convinced of that, but a real person. He will slip off this afternoon, while Lucy sleeps, as she surely will, she is so lethargic lately; he must know, before they leave. He would always regret not knowing who—man or woman, native or white man—has acted so playfully with them during their time here. He cannot leave without knowing; even now, the island draws him, taunts him, its trees reach for him, enticing him with their secrets.

I have slept long, and feel rested now. I remember: the girl on the beach—have I told her the story? Fred's story; it hurts less today, for the telling. I can almost smile with tenderness for what was, after all, so long ago. My visitors, with their new ways and their youth, remind me of the passing of time—this too helps. Time has its uses, after all; time builds a reef against the pounding of remembrance.

Why did I choose to live, when he was gone? Why did I not follow him beyond the reef to the east, to close the circle?

Because if I did that, who would bear witness? Who—still alive, still loving—would carry the burden of memory?

I live on, even if no one knows it but I. He stays by me, in my thoughts and my dreams, in the daily measure of memory.

Iowawa.

I think about the girl and I am sad—she does not know how to cherish her husband, she does not know about the regret of lost months turning into years. Because she is—as I was, long ago—certain of her, of their, immortality. She has no fear that on her next passage she might be lost overboard, that he may be struck by a swinging boom. I flew with danger, great danger, and I knew it, yet I too felt immune, protected.

Who, of Lucy and Robin, does not love enough? Who does not wake in the morning as if it were the last day; who does not wake and know that even one day of life is good and meaningful because the other one is there?

It is cooler today, overcast with the arrival of tropical winter. There will be rain, and gales, sweeping across my flat domain; at times the wind is so strong I imagine the island will tear free from its coral roots and drift wildly at sea.

They have been running their engine; again it purrs and hums and they will prepare to leave. Today is my last chance, then; soon their sails will fill and fade into blue, taking them back into their familiar world.

I look at my hands. They are strong and sinewy and barely marked, but when I tried to leave with the sailboat, when I was locked into that stifling sail cupboard, they became stiff and tired, and were spattered with the spots of age.

How long would I last, out there? How long before I would shrivel and slump and grow deaf and incontinent? How long before memories would fade into forgetfulness and confusion?

I tremble with the island at the approaching storm, still far out to sea. After all these years alone I have grown afraid of decisions.

The man Robin sits on the side of his rubber boat, frowning, thoughtful. With a stick he draws idly in the sand, he looks from side to side, defiant and puzzled at the same time. He is uncomfortable and restless, a person waiting. He has not come to the island for its sake; he has come here to get away from his boat, or to find something here.

I sense he is looking for me. Men like to know; they cannot abide mysteries.

I stand a few hundred feet away, hidden behind the latticework of tree trunks. He raises his eyes and looks right at me, through me, and beyond. What does this tell me about his quest for knowledge?

Now he is walking, with the dogged step of the white hunter, and I follow, dancing lightly. I feel playful, a sprite. He looks ahead, and I am behind, a silent shadow.

I follow him the length of the western shore; then he turns and begins to crisscross the island, lifting undergrowth as he passes, to look beneath. Sometimes he pauses to feel the ground; on his knees he swings his head from side to side along the low earth, like a querying animal. But I remain behind and above him, he does not look my way.

He mutters to himself but I cannot hear his words, yet I can smell his anger—a trace he leaves on the air with his human, strong, man's smell; with the gruff timber of his voice.

I try to reach through time and see him as a man, as I saw Fred. I wonder if there is desire left in me, after all these years, or if desire has always been a part of something greater. I cannot imagine it for this man. He is like a child, despite his height, his well-trimmed beard. His body is polished not through hard work and hard living as Fred's was but is maintained, I suspect, by health and ease alone.

He grows tired after half the island has been searched; he stops to lie on the beach near the cove. He sleeps. While he sleeps I bring him a coconut, husked and opened, ready to eat.

Upon waking he finds the nut and hurls it, furious, into the waves. "I'll find you, you game-playing aborigine!" he shouts, legs widespread and fists clenched; I laugh from behind my trees.

And although I know his anger and his threat, this is good fun to me because I am both outside and inside the fiction. I look in from without and I see the plot unfolding as only the author and reader can, as a rule; the characters—in novels as in real life—are confined to their role, forced to play, blindly, assigned to their fate. He searches, so puzzled by his invisible opponent; I watch him search, make him search, become the author of my own story.

I have indeed grown far apart from my own kind, to take pleasure in mocking and tormenting them, rather than entering into speech and exchange. Have I gone mad, or is it because I suspect that they would not understand me? I am no longer as they once knew me—still know me—from their newspapers and newsreels. I have grown wild and free, more animal or fairy in my aboriginal heart.

And they are so touchingly, doggedly determined as they sit on their boat in the shelter of the lagoon—determined to find, to fix, to love. Their will is so strong, it negates the natural flow; it is like the drought, drying up the spring.

He walks again, a determined rage to the set of his jaw. He has found a big long branch and with it he jabs at the undergrowth. He pauses as his stick knocks against something, sending back a dull echo of wood. He bends over, shuffles among the leaves and branches, lifts an object to the light. I recognize the old sundial, warped and eroded; he holds it in his hands and does not seem to know what it is. The sun is hidden, but a strange light from some other source catches the warped shaft and sends a long pencil of gray shadow onto his arm, snakelike. He starts, then drops the dial as if it had burned him.

Now he no longer follows a regular, well-laid pattern, but strides in an angry serpentine, hoping to find by chance what is actually just behind him.

But there is the shelter; he will find the shelter, eventually, if his determination leads him there. I hesitate to run to it and hide some of my belongings, and the things I stole from them, but we are now so near, he might discover me.

At dusk—I sense rather than see that it is dusk, for all day we have wandered in a shadowless gloom—he finds the shelter. A cry of triumph, rehearsed, theatrical, for him alone: "Aha!" I hear him rummaging in the tea chest, I hear him brushing aside the entrance to the shelter, fumbling on the ground in the shelter where I keep all the small things Fred made, now worn and fragile. I worry that he might break something with his big angry paws. I find a hiding place and wait. The wind is rising.

$\mathcal{L}$ucy wakes from a long sleep with drugged reluctance. Her talk with Robin will be unpleasant. She fears that once again he will try to avoid conflict, retreating behind a fortress of silence, armed only with his small glass of whiskey or brandy. She wants to get it over with—the preemptive strike, the surprise attack—because she fears his reaction and is no longer able to live in uncertainty.

The child is there, growing inside her; it too demands an answer.

Robin decides to wait by the shelter. Soon it will be night, the ghost must return. In the meantime he will explore the primitive domesticity of the place. He finds rough-hewn utensils and bowls, spoons and dull-bladed wooden knives, crooked plates much scored by the blade of a sharper knife. He glances into the shelter. Small carved animals parade against the backdrop of palm leaf. Dolphins, sharks, ordinary fish, an awkward whale, out of scale with the others. Then a cat, in perpetual pursuit of a tiny mouse. Finally, an airplane, primitive yet smooth with handling. All stand suspended in creation by the hand of the one who made them, who must look at them every day, perhaps play with them—strange luxury for such a primitive condition.

The cat and mouse—surely not native to these islands? Robin's heart pounds, he feels light-headed with the triumph of discovery, with the anticipation of mystery soon unveiled. He touches nothing, yet peers and wonders. The animals, the utensils, and now a ragged pile of worn clothing. Next to the shelter there is a water-warped tea chest turned on its side; Robin can just make out the name of the Chinese city whose tea it once carried. Inside the chest are old, water-logged volumes, their covers curled with damp and splattered with stains of time. He reaches into the chest, hesitant, looking at his fingertips. Then he remembers that the ghost was not so circumspect when intruding upon *Stowaway*.

The books are very old sight reduction tables, barely legible. Robin watches in horror as the next book he picks up disintegrates in his hand, its binding split, its pages crumbling, frail leaves upon the warm earth. He recognizes the columns and hours of the almanac before the rising wind scuttles the pages away into the undergrowth. He grabs at scraps of paper, ineffectually, curiously embarrassed, as if he were being watched. He is not as clever at intruding upon other people's things as the ghost is.

But ghost no more, he mutters; these books are the proof that the island's inhabitant must have been shipwrecked here, a long time ago; also proof that he must come from a Western country. Hence the cat and mouse; hence the airplane.

Robin places the shreds of paper into the binding and shoves the book back in place as best he can. Hurriedly, he explores the rest of the small homestead. In the shelter, under the pile of clothes, lies his own missing paperback; next to it is a pile of writing paper, too new to be anyone's but their own. So there are things they have not even missed; he finds a roll of toilet paper, some pencils. In a corner behind a pile of coconuts stands the jar of raspberry jam.

Holding the writing paper, Robin crawls back out into the fading light. He squints at the handwriting: small and crabbed, it works its way across the page. He begins to read: "I dream that I am flying again . . ." but is interrupted when a gust of wind lifts the paper and threatens to blow it away. Robin hastily reassembles the pile and returns it to the safety of the shelter. He had not noticed the strength of the wind; the trees now dance and taunt him. Wait, or be too late?

In a moment of urgent hesitation, a chance he knows may never be given to him again, he reaches for one of the small sculptures and shoves it deep into the pocket of his shorts.

*

Lucy has taken her notebook and is writing, but she cannot find a flow. Her letters stop and start and jerk across the page. She must write of this desolate crossroads in her life, of her confusion and solitude. Can the scrawled words make it all come clear, somehow?

She writes:

> He's not here, he's left me alone and gone off again, to look for the person-thing-ghost on the island. He is more concerned in finding an answer to this puzzle than a solution to our problems . . . what solution? Can there ever be one—why is so much time spent trying to fix things between people, as if one could fix emotions and disappointment and just plain everyday boredom . . . as if this child could fix our marriage, as people often believe.
>
> I don't want it, I cannot be tied down . . .

She lifts her head for a moment and listens; new sounds startle her from her thoughts. A whistling, high-pitched: the wind through the stainless steel rigging. Then a creak and a thump: the anchor chain pulling against the bow of the boat.

She leaves her notebook and hurries on deck. Darkening clouds now scud across the lighter gray of the sky; the lagoon is a wind-pocked surface of fast-moving ripples. *Stowaway* has begun to toss in the wind. This is not new to Lucy, but it is for here. She looks to shore. The dinghy waits, but there is no sign of Robin.

Worry rises, from a sickening weakness in her stomach to an acrid taste upon her tongue. Strong wind at anchor means danger, and she knows this. Several times in the past, strong wind has caused their anchor to drag along the bottom, moving *Stowaway* towards shore, other boats, rocks. If it should begin to drag here, they will go onto the beach and have no way of getting off again. Lucy knows she must do something to prevent this, but her options are limited.

She looks again to the beach: the palm trees are dancing wildly. If she had the dinghy, she could attach the outboard and, with the added power, ferry a second anchor out into the lagoon from the bow of the boat. She has the outboard, but no dinghy.

But there is the engine, of course! Now they have the engine, she can start it and keep the boat motoring gently forward against the wind and chop, away from shore.

She runs to the hook where the engine key is kept, but there is nothing there. A picture returns to her from earlier that day: Robin, smiling and satisfied, waving the key in front of her, then slipping it into the pocket of his shorts, casually oblivious of the importance his gesture would assume only a few hours later, casually oblivious of his own carelessness in leaving her in such danger.

Another option is to sail off the anchor and out to sea, something so dangerous, she could not possibly attempt it alone.

Finally, she can simply drop a second anchor and hope it will bite where she drops it, should the primary one fail. This she can do, and she will watch all the while for any change in their position.

Lucy releases the lanyard which holds the second anchor in place on the bowsprit and readies the windlass to let it down. She feels cold, for the first time in weeks: cold from the wind, cold from a new and very present fear. The sound of chain running through the windlass reassures her, briefly. She is doing what she can, but she must do more.

Where is he?

Night is closing round as Robin runs towards the lagoon. He reaches into his pocket to make sure of the presence of the soft wooden sculpture, but his fingers curl around the cold metal of the engine key. The first drops of rain are tossed like pebbles against his cheeks and legs as he runs. The wind pushes against him as if to say, go back to the shelter! too late! too late! The trees stand upright against their natural inclination towards the lagoon;

the younger ones bend backward, aching in their ignorance of storms.

A short, wind-driven chop is building in the lagoon. *Stowaway* bounces, clanking her anchor chain as she rides. Lucy waits by the cockpit and feels the first drops of rain. The contours of the island are fading in the darkness. Soon the beach too will disappear into the night. Moon and stars are hidden by cloud.

Robin will not be able to see the boat in the darkness, so she hurries below to switch on the anchor light to guide him back.

How will she know, in this darkness, if the boat is dragging towards the shore, until it is too late?

Robin is in the dinghy, rowing hard against the waves. He sees Lucy's light and strains his back, his arms, all his thoughts towards that light. Water splashes over the bow of the small boat, surprisingly cold, as if the deeper ocean had forced its way into the lagoon. Robin rows incessantly, but draws no closer to the bobbing light.

Lucy squints into the darkness. Perhaps it is movement she can see by the beach in the faint glow of the anchor light: the yellow stripe on the body of the inflatable dinghy, leaving the shore. Yes, she thinks, he's coming! We'll be all right! Then, after some minutes, when she does not see him, her fear suggests that *Stowaway* is dragging already, moving closer to shore.

She stumbles forward to feel the anchor chain. She is not sure of this, but thinks that a throbbing, vibrating chain means dragging; a chain which is taut means the anchor is holding.

The chain is tight, rigid. For now. She clings to this hope.

Is this vagabonding, weather-governed life too hard for Lucy, too fraught with danger after all? She suspects she is not strong enough physically and is therefore too dependent upon Robin. This has skewed the once-easy nature of their relationship. As she waits in the shelter of the dodger under the heavy starless sky, her fear pivots from storms to unborn children. She does not want a child, not now, if ever; the storm, her solitude and her anxiety merely confirm this.

Are you there, unborn child, she asks; do you see how your mother is alone and helpless at this time, and how the very thought of you makes her sick with anger? Do you see how your father is absent when he is needed? Is this a world you want to come into?

Chilled, she goes below for a jacket. When she returns she searches the darkness for the yellow stripe but there is nothing; she calls his name, but hears no reply.

Robin hears her calling but cannot answer; his voice is taken from him in the exhaustion of the struggle to row. He is making no progress towards the boat. All his strength is as nothing against this wind.

He wonders if he could swim. He would try, but he is so tired, already; then there are the sharks, and Lucy's concern. He had promised . . . but now which is the greater risk, the greater danger? Is she all right? Is the anchor holding?

He will swim if he sees the light move; for now he will return to shore to rest and to watch. His own immobility will tell him if *Stowaway*'s light draws nearer to shore.

Lucy drifts to and from the edge of sleep, roused now and again by the lurch of the boat against the anchor chain, or by a sudden burst of rain from the invisible sky. In this peripheral zone of consciousness her thoughts go very clear and very deep; no subtleties or illusions can survive in these latitudes. Her misery is simple and brutal, casting a cold, storm-lit clarity upon the imprisoning island of her own self-delusion. She believed herself to be happy with Robin, she believed in their future together, in their shared adventure. The child and the island have changed all that; she does not know if she can pretend anymore and wait for a gradual, hard-won change in her marriage. Something inside her has ceased to feel, walled up behind her inexplicable anger; her body, too, has grown silent, numbed by habit and willful coercion. When, how did this happen? How did she lose touch with her body, to become so careless, so unaware, that this foreign child was able to enter against her will? An accident, it is often whispered about unwanted children; she does not want her child to be an accident.

She no longer belongs to her body. She has become detached, a governing mind, a voice commanding her body, mostly to resist; sometimes, dutifully, to take its pleasure. And now this other thing is happening, over which she has had no control. Well, I can fix that, she thinks stubbornly, I control my destiny, and I don't want this child, it's ill-conceived, under a bad sky full of bad portent.

Stowaway lunges and rears, the rigging shakes, quaking the mast down to the depths of the keel. The wheel strains against some invisible helmsman. Lucy starts and runs up on deck, to the bow. Her eyes strain against the black water, as if her will could allow her to see through it, as if she could see the coral bed where their primary anchor, with its forty pounds of steel and all its chain, has just shifted its feeble grip some six feet closer to shore.

$\mathcal{T}$he dolphin is gone. How could he show such cruelty towards an old woman and her few treasures?

But he does not know I am an old woman; if he did, his laughter would resound from here to Hawaii. He must believe I am a monster, a cannibal, no doubt, larger than life and full of evil intentions towards him and his wife. I only wanted to help, to observe, perhaps to travel with them, but there is no trust possible with this arrogant man.

Fred's dolphin. One of the last things he carved. It was meant to be a toy.

I sit in my dripping, shaking shelter and listen to the noise of the storm. There have been many such storms. The island groans and thrashes, but it is so young; with dawn it will stretch and shake itself like a dog, then relax once more against the shoulder of the sea. I expect this, and wait in my shelter as it shivers like the cockpit of some imaginary aircraft.

This storm is different from others because the boat in the lagoon is in danger. I followed Robin to the shore—he could not row against the waves which threaten his home. I hesitated to help him, but once again did not want to reveal myself. Now, because of the dolphin, I am glad I did not. He cursed and pounded with his fist in rage against the wet sand. The dim light atop the mainmast carved a blurred arc of light against the pitch night, like a drunken star. I was cold. I returned to the shelter and found the dolphin gone.

Thus I rediscover the dark weakness of the human heart.

Rain drums on the frail roof of the shelter; wind pours through the walls and brings me the mournful sounds of the sailboat's struggle. From the depths of the lagoon I hear the dull metallic scrape of the two anchors as they try to dig into the hostile coral; the clang of the chain as it rides up and down in the surge. I hear the slatting of the booms as the boat rocks, the shriek of the wind in the wire rigging, keening, like the clairvoyant ghosts of long-ago Kuma's stories, as they flew above the thatched roofs I shall never see. But loudest of all I hear the girl's voice, her distress, her misery. She is talking to her unborn child, cursing its father, cursing its existence. Her words are bitter as mine never were; she seems to cherish neither child nor husband, and cares only for her own safety in the storm. Does she know how easily she could lose everything?

But she is young, the age I was when . . . She knows so little of hardship; she thinks she is unhappy—what does she know of suffering! Does she know that there are some things which simply cannot be remembered, which are effaced by pain?

Yet for her sake I will try to remember, because I want to save her, before it is too late.

For now, the anchor holds.

$\mathcal{I}$ lost the will to live, after Fred was gone: for days I lay without moving on my pallet, drinking only the stagnant water which lay in a bowl I had prepared, days before, for him. Only sleep gave me some release; when awake I stared at the thin walls of the shelter just as he must have done during his illness. I stared at the shifting spots of light, the pale motes of dust swirling in their own separate galaxy. My universe became as small as that, reduced to the contemplation of a mote of dust.

But I did not account for life's tenacity. I refused to think of the child, still there, who would not be dislodged by mental suffering; the child who no doubt knew of its father's death in some strange way, who might be born short or ugly or even beautiful, but never ordinary, in reflection of this disaster of its embryonic life.

Such thoughts gradually aroused me, and I walked out from the shelter on a day washed fresh and bright with the briskness of the trade winds. I sat for a long time by the lagoon and thought that I must decide, quickly, whether I had the courage to go on, to stay alive for the sake of the child. I did not know what Fred would have me do; I did not really believe in an afterlife for lovers.

I walked slowly into the lagoon and lay back against the pillow of water, and floated aimlessly in reflection of the flocculent clouds overhead. Well-being—pure, physical well-being—came over me, telling me I was a healthy woman, telling me that my body still wanted me to bear this child and that it was Nature's child, not mine, to decide about. I lay in the water and put my hand on my belly and felt the hardness of growth, the determination of life. I stood and walked from the lagoon. Something in me changed at that moment, a parting of darkness to let in a pinprick of light. Embryonic hope; the discovery that there might, still, be a reason for living. For Fred's sake, for the child's sake. Because Nature willed it.

For the first time in days, as I stepped from the water, I glimpsed my reflection: my hair was the color of ashes.

I talked to the child, after that, endlessly, caressingly, as if my words could be a balm to my own loss, to the child's fatherlessness. I nourished her with tears, but she returned my blood with hope.

I took her flying. We returned to Paramaribo, to Fortaleza, to Karachi. I told her of all the places I had been and the people I had met. I told her about her father, about the good times, and the bad. I did not hide who he had been, before the island, but mostly I told her about the father she would have known. Through the telling I saw him differently, saw the promise of the man he would become on the island, and it was like finding a secret trove of memories.

So we managed for a time, protected from darker sorrows by tales of the past. I began to fish on my own and did not do badly—the lagoon took pity on me and surrendered its fruits willingly. I talked to the child, and together we ate and lay in the shelter where, before sleep, I would try to remember the lullabies of my childhood.

How absurd, to tell stories and sing lullabies to an unborn child.

I did not make a cradle. I would have the cradle of my arms, too long empty, to hold the child when she came.

$\mathcal{R}$obin lies against the cold flank of the dinghy. He is soaked through, and cold, and sick with apprehension. He wonders about the wrath of islands; he wonders if his determination to confront their spirits has brought on this retribution. He does not believe in such things, normally; but nothing is normal anymore, and there is a moment's relief in attributing misfortune to higher causes.

From time to time he raises his head to look for the anchor light, to assure himself of its presence in the same unmoving spot in the darkness. The downpour drives away all notions of boundaries, horizons, points of reference, yet he knows where that light must be, whence it must not move. It is like a beacon of safety, a madman's lighthouse.

In the long-ago days when their early navigation took them through crowded shipping lanes at night, they would sometimes keep watch in just such a way, dozing for seconds, sometimes minutes, before springing up to check the horizon for lights that signaled the presence of a ship. The light, the ship, spelled danger for as long as it approached; then it would recede on the curve of its journey, like a star casually circling out of orbit. At that time, relief was in movement; now safety lies in immobility.

Once, during the night, in his tense wakefulness that slips into sleep now and again, Robin imagines that the light is moving towards shore. He jumps up out of the dinghy and runs to the water's edge, then, as he watches more carefully, he sees that it has not moved, that his fatigue is playing with him. He returns to the dinghy and curls up against its cold rubber surface, trying to retrieve whatever warmth he might have left there.

Lucy sits in her sleeping bag, impotent against her shivering. She knows it is not the cold. The shivering will not stop until day breaks, or the wind drops, or Robin returns. She has no thoughts, only fractured images and intense concentration upon her plight.

Now and again the boat shudders or rolls in the wind; halyards slap against the mast.

She closes her eyes and lets fatigue take her to a place that is neither waking nor sleeping, but that is full of dreams. The child is speaking to her, not in words but in silent pictures of entreaty. A hillside of sharp, intense color, green bleeding into blue, dazzling in the sunlight. At the top of the hill, a spot of red. It is a child's sweater; Lucy cannot see whether the child is a boy or a girl. A bearded man is holding the child's hand; the man, she knows, is not Robin. He is too tall, thinner, darker. The child is saying, without speaking, My father is sad. Lucy knows his eyes must be deep and haunted, although she cannot see them. The man and the child wait for her, waving, their hands huge against the clouds. Lucy stands at the bottom of the hill, she wants to come up, but her feet will not move. She waits, rooted; the child is crying out to her, "Mama! Ma-ma!" The man slowly lifts away from the hillside into the blue-black sky; now Lucy begins to run, struggling against the thick grass. When she arrives on the crown of the hill, the child is gone, but has left the small red sweater behind. Lucy looks at it, too frightened to pick it up, but thinks, The child will be cold.

The chain strains and threatens to snap the bowsprit. Lucy does not know this; she wakes and sees the darkness and tries to turn the intensity of her fear and shivering to prayer. But she knows that this is a false security, a momentary reprieve. Because the child has not finished speaking to her. Sleep takes her again and this time the child shows her the island, as if from the height of a cloud or an airplane. There is the familiar palm-studded crescent against the deep blue of the sea. They drop lower, and Lucy sees a woman standing alone on the back of the crescent, gazing out across the ocean. Lucy cannot see her face, but she knows she is crying, for her tears swell the tide. The beaches are submerged; waves curl against the base of the trees.

$\mathcal{S}$ome stories need no telling. You know the rest. You know that there is no child, that she was never born to me a live, breathing being. You know that only days after Fred's leaving, in one predawn awakening, a pain came upon my body such as I had never before experienced, pain that roused me from the illusion of sleep and well-being; pain, at last, commensurate with the intensity of loss. Almost a liberating pain. I lay on the pallet and shivered with fear, now doubled up with my knees against my chin, now stretched out as if I could find my way out of the pain. How long did it last? Such things are not measured in minutes and hours, but in the passage from future to past, from hope to bitterness. I did not care what happened to me, once I knew; I hoped for release—and if that meant death, then I was not afraid.

When the stabbing pain stopped, it left me deep inside the dark cave opened up by my first loss, the cave on whose threshold I still dwell.

You know that for forty years I have lived alone on this island and have come, after a long apprenticeship, to excel at solitude, because what I have lost of human society has been replaced by Nature, a society unto itself; because the island needs me to be the recipient of its gifts and the lover of its secret ways. In return I have not aged; in return I have been allowed to transgress the very laws of Nature. In the country of my birth I would be a freak; here I belong, and have my place among the palm trees and the pandanus and the flowering hibiscus; in the waters of the lagoon; under the stars.

Such solitude is not for many. Who would ever choose to forgo the pleasures of humanity: the embrace of a lover, the resonant serenity of motherhood? I did not choose—exile was thrust upon me, lover and child wrenched from me. Has survival, in the long run, been a blessing?

Perhaps that is not for me to say. My existence is made of other things now, and I have learned to be content with them. Sand and waves, wind and clouds. Ethereal, yet eternal, things.

*L*ucy awakes with a start. Something has entered her thoughts, unbidden, like an intruder. The wrath of God. Are there deals to be made? Can she negotiate the life of her unborn child in exchange for her fear? Take my fear, O Lord, and I will take your child and bring it to the light?

She is not religious but she is shocked by the implication of her thoughts, and their conclusion. For a moment she finds relief from fear, until the wind brings her back to the lagoon. Up on deck, nothing has changed; the storm is getting worse. She makes her way to the stern of the boat and squints into the darkness in the direction of the beach, but she can see nothing. The rain drums on her back and neck through the foul-weather jacket; her legs are bare and shivering. *Stowaway* rides the small steep waves whipped up by the storm, tugging at anchor chain and rode.

A sudden gust drives the boat closer to the invisible shore; with it comes a noise, not loud against the shrieking of the wind, but terrible, because it comes from the boat. Lucy crawls forward and shines the beam of her flashlight against the bowsprit: the bronze roller which leads the anchor and chain away from the bow and into the water has been pulled down and away from the bowsprit, and hangs loosely on its bolts. A terrible crack has begun to split the wooden bowsprit. Lucy cannot see the damage in detail; at this moment mere damage does not matter. The chain lies straining with its thousands of pounds against a few loosened bolts, against the softness of wood, before the next stage which might rip the anchor and chain from the boat altogether.

She shines a light on the anchor rode of the second anchor: the rope is so thin compared to chain, so fragile in coral, like thread. It is taut now, where it hung slack before. The boat has surely moved.

*

Robin sees Lucy's small light moving through the rain, a mere thumbprint of white against the darkness. Is something wrong? Why is she checking on deck? What can she do against the mindless strength of the wind?

Yet he is comforted that she is trying; it is more than he can do, stranded on the beach by his own stupidity. Events may have conspired against him—this is what he would like to believe—but if *Stowaway* is driven onto the beach, he will be no less responsible than the wind.

Lucy's light moves along the deck, then disappears, leaving the night darker than ever.

In all his life he has never known such a time as this: the waiting, the fear. They could lose their home, everything, and be bound to the island as hopelessly and irrevocably as the damned islander, who might well be the cause of their present troubles. If the islander had been open and friendly and not behaved like a damned ghost, leading Robin away from the boat at a crucial time, he might be there helping them now—

Robin springs to his feet and begins to move through the trees, shouting wildly, pushing against the madly shaking trunks as if fighting his way into hell itself. He will seek him out, grab him by the neck if need be, drag him to shore, make him pay for his tricks and deception. The islander *will* help; together, they can row to the boat and help Lucy; they will be able to start the engine. Robin plunges into the blackness, into the island itself, all fear gone, led by the blind light of his own determination.

$\mathcal{I}$ have extraordinary vision in this darkness; I see through the folds of night and rain to the boat, where the girl stands, now mindless of the storm, her fear pouring with her tears into the lagoon. I can see through the turbulent thickness of the water, to where one anchor has a tentative grip against the coral, to where the other, more fortunate, has dug into the sand but is held by only a short length of chain and then by too-fragile rope, even now rubbing against an outcrop of coral.

I can hear a voice, too, a man's voice, crying against the strained harmonies of the storm.

I can help you, foolish man, but only by helping your wife. I will not help you. You can wander and search all you like, you will not find me to help you.

No one helped me when I had lost the child. I lay for days in my own blood and marveled at the stubbornness of life. I seemed to be waiting, hoping for it all to end, hoping that I would die sweetly in my sleep, or be struck by lightning.

But I never thought, that time, about taking my life. It must be that I had survived so well, for so long, that the will to live—not mine, my body's—was stronger than anything. At times I despised this strong body of mine—never strong in the past, always sick with something, or so tired and run down—which must have wanted so badly to eat and run and swim and show its useless strength under this broiling sun; it was so eager to show its defiance, its newfound perfection. It refused to weaken or die; it wanted, still, to share a man's love, to have babies.

Empty vessel for survival. What of my soul? Perhaps my soul had gone into a long sleep—but then I would no longer feel, or care; my soul was sick, and would get better. If my body could survive, so must my soul.

I lay in the shelter and let the days pass, long stretches of road through the dun-colored hinterland of existence. How long I journeyed there I do not know, but one day I arrived at a small clearing where a few struggling flowers grew. I raised my face to the wind. Never again would I raise my fists in triumph and say, "It's grand to be alive!" But I would learn, with the seabirds and ocean creatures who were now my companions, to affirm, "I am alive."

Thus I have learned, too, how to shut off my mind when it becomes impatient or demanding. I sit with the serenity of lions in the bush, paws outstretched, observant and calm.

I am sad for the girl on the boat; she has so much but fails to see. Her mind is like the thickness of storm, driving out all chance for peace.

She may never have another chance. I never did.

I hear her praying, in desperation, as I once did. Because she is afraid of the storm—afraid for the boat, afraid that if it is lost, she will be lost. I hear her making strange deals with God, as I once did.

I sometimes wonder if God honored my bargain, after all. If on a blustery day somewhere several leagues to the east a ship passed on its route to San Francisco, or a small outrigger homeward bound . . .

This is why I refuse to believe. If God existed, he could not be so cruel.

How can I tell the girl she will not lose all by being stranded here?

But for a long time I thought I had lost everything, twice, three times—it has taken many storms for me to learn otherwise.

I make my way through the dripping, groaning trees to the lagoon. My eyes are blind in this darkness; I find my way through years of familiarity with the island. What I have seen tonight of danger and despair draw me to the yacht as to a beacon. I must help her.

$\mathcal{L}$ucy has surrendered to her imagination. She sits by the navigation station and prepares her message, brief and desperate, then she lifts the handset of the radio.

"Mayday, Mayday, Mayday, this is the yacht *Stowaway*, we are in grave danger. Repeat: grave danger. Can anyone hear me?"

She gives no position and ignores the fact that her life is not in immediate danger; but like Robin she knows they could be shipwrecked, and sensibly she realizes this may be her last chance to send out a radio message. The engine compartment will flood, the batteries will be lost, the radio will be dead.

Calmly, as if watching the approach of a fire still far on the horizon, she gathers a few small things she wants to save: her notebook, some jewelry, some photos, the volume of Shakespeare. She takes their emergency bag with its supply of water, flares, first aid, fishing tackle, matches and emergency rations, and adds her personal things to the bag.

Meanwhile, the radio returns only silence; Lucy tries again. She must try. To be swallowed unheard by this hiccup in time is more frightening than the possible loss of the boat.

She changes into dry clothing and opens a tin of fruit. Outside, the wind continues its horrible keening. Lucy tries not to listen, but the rhythmic banging of the anchor chain punctuates her struggle with fear. When she calls on the radio, she feels better; hope drives her, until five minutes of silence have elapsed and her anxiety peaks again. There seems to be no end to it. No one ever tells you this; they say things like "Nothing to fear but fear itself," but they never tell you that fear suspends time, like some ghastly approximation of the hereafter.

To keep busy and to fuel hope, she looks for a spare engine key. She marvels that they have been such organized, careful sailors in some respects—safety, supplies—and so careless and amateurish in others. A spare key should be labeled and hanging on a special hook, but if it is anywhere to be found at this critical time, it will be in a drawer with assorted nuts, bolts, screws, dead fuses, transistor batteries, broken pencils, stray fluffs of caulking cotton, rusty drill bits. She empties drawer after drawer upon the cabin sole under the dim light of the oil lamp; everything goes rolling away almost before she has a chance to see what is there.

When she has finished with the drawers she turns to Robin's locker, visualizing a key tucked, perhaps, in one of his pockets. She takes out every jacket, T-shirt, pair of shorts or jeans and searches every pocket; while she searches, the rattle of the contents of emptied drawers continues—forward, aft, starboard, port—with the restless yawing of the boat. Here in the forward cabin she can hear the awful clanking of the anchor chain, the dull groan of the rode rubbing in its chock; at least they are holding. She dare no longer go to check; there is nothing more she can do.

Once, the boat heels and groans, then jerks abruptly with a loud thud; Lucy cries out, certain this is the end. But the noise is not repeated; it is almost as if a stillness has followed, and she can hear the pounding of her heart more clearly now.

She empties more drawers and lockers, to find nothing. A stray screw causes her to fall awkwardly to the floor, hitting her head on the table. She surrenders to circumstance, curled against the table leg, her nose close to the oily smell of bilgewater. So much easier, finally, to give in, to lie there enumerating frustrations and misfortunes, to give in to tears, to cry, to do nothing. Is this why armies surrender? Does it ease the suffering, the fear?

Robin plunges on through what has become a jungle of darkness and wet, thrashing undergrowth. He has nothing but intuition and a vague sense of direction to guide him to the spot he found with such difficulty by daylight. He shouts and pleads, his voice carries feebly on the wind. He thinks ruefully of the alleged telepathic abilities of certain aboriginal populations. Why can't their islander find him, then?

In the darkness he does not see the tangled skein of undergrowth waiting in his path; he stumbles suddenly, violently. An intense pain shoots up his leg. On the wet ground, cursing and shouting and holding his ankle, he is caught like a rabbit in a trap; he can no longer save anyone. He tries to stand, but cannot; he can only lie in this mad jungle of storm and brutish Nature, waiting for daybreak. Then, humiliated and reduced, he will crawl back to what might remain of his dream.

The lamp in the dark cabin grows dimmer. It is nearly out of oil. Lucy lies on the cabin sole, shivering. She does not know how long she has been there; her watch, its glass now cracked from the fall, tells her that there is only half an hour at most until first light. Sometimes the wind drops after dawn. Perhaps it's nearly over, she tells herself, last words of encouragement. But the storm still rages on the edges of her consciousness: the gunshot peppering of the rain on deck, the doleful complaint of the wind, the wash of waves against the hull. She drifts to the shore of sleep, past caring.

The flame flickers on its dry wick, the light dies. The darkness calls her back and she sits up. The rattling against the cabin sole has stopped. The boat seems very still, but the wind continues its shrill song in the rigging. Lucy stands up, stiff and sticky with fatigue, and climbs through the companionway.

The dawn is a thick slate-gray, smeared with the residue of storm and the saturated colors of rainfall. But the rain has stopped, and *Stowaway* sits on a small patch of lagoon whose surface is as smooth and opaque as that of a pond in winter. The wind bays in protest, and Lucy can just make out the furious white spray on the reef. The wind lifts her hair, chilling her skin; she can see small whitecaps now in the lagoon itself. Yet *Stowaway* sits on, serene and absolutely calm, like some mother hen upon her eggs, as if there were no wind to ruffle her feathers. On the island—closer now, of that Lucy is certain—the palm trees still writhe furiously against the dark sky.

Lucy rushes forward to the anchor. The chain hangs lifeless, as on the calmest day in a currentless bay; the rode sways gently to the motion she herself has caused.

Is this the eye of the hurricane; are they now about to be blown out to the reef and more certain disaster? She watches as the night fades and a setting star shows briefly between the cloud cover and the blurred horizon; she watches and the boat does not move, and the island comes no closer.

On the beach there is a pale silhouette against the trees. She calls, furiously, "Robin! Robin!" but the figure disappears, melting into the darkness which still has hold of the island.

*D*id I calm the waters of the lagoon, or merely lead the girl into sleep beyond the worst of the storm? Are these not the same thing, in another reality?

I stood and watched the sailboat until the worst was over, until with dawn the wind gave up and shrugged out to sea. I could see in the subsiding waters of the lagoon that the anchors had bitten in, and I knew that later that day Robin would have to dive to disentangle one of them from a vise of growth and coral. I was tired from my vigilance, and turned for home.

On the way I found him, asleep against the base of the palm trees. He lay curled with his arms around his left leg; I could see his ankle was swollen. He had lost, in sleep, all arrogance; his cheeks were flushed beneath the mad tangle of his rain-soaked hair. Before he could wake I fashioned a bandage of leaves and flower petals—scattered everywhere by the storm—and wrapped it quickly around his ankle.

When I had finished I allowed myself one small indulgence, one small mad gesture. I bent over his lips, and took from them the forgotten savor of man, youth, lovemaking—a taste of the earth, like a wine long aged in a dark, damp cellar.

Now I lie tired in my shelter, holding Fred's dolphin to my chest. I lifted it from Robin's pocket as he slept; he made a gesture of protest and nearly woke, then turned back against the soft earth. The anger ebbed from me as I watched his sleeping face, as I remembered other sleeping faces.

Let them leave now, to return to the existence they understand; I will stay with mine.

*R*obin awakes. His cheek is burning; the sun has found its way through the screen of trees to light this small patch of skin. He is confused by daylight and brings into waking the illusory mood of fairy tales—the long sleep, the waking in an unknown forest.

Around him the foliage drips with the rich contentment of morning after storm; the wind has died. He stands, takes a step forward, and finds his ankle will bear his weight, because it is supported by a curious brace of leaves and petals. At first he wants to tear it off, but it is bound so tightly that it causes him unnecessary pain in the attempt.

He makes his way slowly through the dripping palms to the lagoon. His heart pounds in rhythm to the throbbing of his ankle. What will he find beyond the trees? What will become of them if they are wrecked, stranded here? Will they be bound by leaves and petals, at the mercy of the islander?

Or will the islander be, at last, at their mercy? Robin stops to consider the islander's fear—how frightened indeed he must be, never to show himself, always leaving offerings, only to find them rejected. It is no wonder he did not come forward to help them during the storm; and yet he stopped to bind Robin's ankle. How did he know it was injured? Had he been following Robin all night? Had he laid a trap for him?

Through the fringe of trees Robin can now see *Stowaway*'s mast, too sickeningly close to shore. He breaks into a limping run, skirting the barrier of trees until he can confirm what he hopes or fears.

He stops abruptly when he reaches the beach and flings his arms towards the sky, as if he could hug the air. The sailboat is very close to shore but sits bobbing at her worn tether, safe, afloat.

He swims the few yards to the boat, mindless of sharks for so short a distance. He climbs the ladder, calling Lucy's name as he climbs. There is no answer. He hurries forward to inspect the anchor chain and sees the damage to the bowsprit; his mind makes a note of it but does not stop. His concern is for Lucy.

He calls again and returns to the companionway. His ankle gives just as he starts down the ladder and with a cry he slides down the ladder onto the cabin floor.

All around him are small sharp pieces of metal, pressing into him where he lies; it is as if the wind had come below to fling open all the drawers, hailing the cabin with the forgotten remnants of all his good intentions, the screws he never sorted, the things which might someday come in handy but which thus far never had. Lucy had often protested, saying that she could never find anything in the drawers when she needed to, so nothing ever got used; she could use the drawers for pens and stamps and souvenirs, if only he would organize things. But he never had, a point of pride or stubbornness. His drawers. He supposes she was looking for the engine key.

Inexplicably, he removes the key from his pocket and leaves it where she will find it, among the rusty nails and broken fuses.

She is sleeping. He watches her, suddenly overwhelmed by tenderness. He had not known until this moment how very close they had been to disaster, how kind Providence has been to him after all. She would have held him in some way responsible; perhaps, as the man, the captain, it was his duty to look after her and the boat. But the surge of feeling has nothing to do with roles or responsibility. It has everything to do with the soft curve of her cheek, bruised pink where it lies against her hand. Nothing else matters beyond the quiet rise and fall of her breathing.

Robin waits a long time while she sleeps. Too exhausted to sleep, he takes the drawers, one by one, and fills them, applying himself carefully to sorting by size and use.

He finds the engine key where he planted it, and puts it back in his pocket, thoughtfully. Why did he want her to share his contrition, his responsibility? But that was before he had seen her sleeping face, the sweep of her hair on the pillow, the corner of her mouth raised in acknowledgment of a dream.

Lucy hears the familiar sound of the coffeepot being opened: twist off the base, knock the grinds into the rubbish, rinse with water . . . She sits up abruptly. Has order been restored so quickly? Was it all some fantastic nightmare—the storm, the anchor, the calm lagoon? She slips out of the berth, stiff with so much sleep and tiredness, and walks to the galley.

Robin pauses with a heaped spoon of coffee as she enters. She has seen him do this hundreds—no, thousands—of times, his elbow raised, his wrist turned inward, but he has never paused, never stopped like that to put the spoon down again, spilling the coffee along the countertop, in order to reshape his elbow and his wrist and catch her somewhere in between, with his arms firm against the small of her back.

They speak of the storm in the lagoon in a language of their own, based on an experience of storms at sea, of lulls, and of a reef. Their vocabulary is now complete; fear needs no translation. Lucy does not tell Robin of the curious calm before dawn, or of the figure on the beach; she feels sure of neither, now. Then she sees the poultice of leaves on Robin's ankle. "How'd you get that?"

"Our friend. I twisted my ankle."

"I didn't notice—"

"It's better now. I should take this off."

"So you found him?"

"No. I found the place where he lives."

"And?"

"He's been there a long time. He speaks English, by the look of it. There were old, worn almanacs and navigation tables. Probably a white man but possibly a native, shipwrecked, most likely. There were some carvings, look—"

Robin reaches into his pocket but finds only the key, which he shows guiltily to Lucy. "I seem to have lost it. I had a carving, of a dolphin. Nice little thing. It's gone. Perhaps he took it back."

Lucy frowns at him indulgently, like a mother whose son confesses to a lie.

"Well, he stole from us. I saw your jam, half a ream of writing paper, toilet paper—"

"Has he got a toilet?" She giggles.

"No, but he has water. There's a small spring near his shelter."

"And you didn't see him?"

Robin shakes his head. "He's too clever by far."

Well, I've seen him, thinks Lucy, but she says nothing. In her first, sleep-blurred memory, the figure on the beach was Robin, but because he failed to respond, because he disappeared into the trees, another figure has taken his place, a mere palimpsest waiting for features to be engraved at some more auspicious time.

The sun has dried the sand and the trees. Only the litter of leaves and petals shows that there has been a storm; only the shower of spray hurling itself against the reef remains of the violence of the waters.

Lucy sits alone. One last time, to watch the sunset, to say goodbye to the island; she and Robin will leave the next day at first light, at the turn of the tide.

She ponders the sudden heaviness of departure. Always, she has wanted to be gone from the island, has wanted to be surrounded once again by other yachts, with their flags of many countries flying in invitation from stern or mizzenmast. She has wanted release from the tension of her shipboard life with Robin; more recently, she has wanted the comfort of airports and telephones and doctors' surgeries.

The child. Conceived in the lagoon, a child of the island. Lucy knows that the storm very nearly left them captive on the island, nearly destroyed their familiar world. She also knows that somehow, in the early, still-dark hours before dawn, they were protected by the island, in an unearthly bay of calm. How she knows this, in the tumult of her memories of rain and wind, and her dream-anguished sleep, is a mystery. But there was a child in those hours, and it spoke to her from a deep, sad place of no return.

She places her hand upon her belly. Is there a slight hardening there, or does she merely imagine it? So early yet—how can one speak of a child, a *baby*—nothing but a comma of flesh, an appendage in her healthy, single body?

But the child is more than flesh, surely, for her to feel so uneasy about its future, about its *life*? This child has existed from the day she met Robin; the seed was planted long ago.

He would be a good father, she knows that; so much of his frustration, affection, even, has deflected upon the boat for lack of a living child. *Stowaway*, their baby, almost lost. How contrite he was, earlier that day, apologizing, begging her forgiveness. The issue was not sin and pardon, but she forgave him.

Superstition, dreams, vague reverie have chased reason from her thoughts. Perhaps she should talk to Robin, appeal to his reason, even if he cannot be unbiased. In this place of signs, can he give her one? Or is she waiting for one from within?

The air is warm, but the wind cools her skin, as if in apology. A small bird hovers questioningly at water's edge, hopping on its sticklike legs, pecking for food or entertainment according to its bird logic. Lucy does not move as the bird sets a course for the spot where her hand presses against the sand. A few hops, a stop to hesitate and ponder, perhaps to judge this huge human being seated on the sand, then, hop-hop, the bird is next to Lucy's hand, attentive, curious. She raises her fingers, slowly, and crosses the few inches to its tiny silken head. The bird submits to her touch, open and trusting. It looks at her as if it knows her, and allows her to stroke its neck, its back, its wings. It is like stroking the lightness of the air itself. Lucy regrets she has no crumbs in her pocket— how hard it must be to find food on the island. Then she smiles and reminds herself that the bird is not in a city park; it is at home here, in its natural habitat.

She holds her breath; the bird inclines its head, then lifts away, abruptly.

Lucy sits for a moment, gently stunned. She has never before caressed a bird, yet this small wild creature came to her and trusted her, where in her understanding of the world such things do not happen. She closes her eyes, to commit to memory. Her eyelashes tingle, her breathing quickens. When she opens her eyes her senses reverberate with the moment; a voice that is her own and yet not quite her own rises on the quiet breathing of the lagoon.

You will see, says the voice. Look again. Look at the sun bleeding into the horizon. Look at the rich amber stain of its passing upon the scene before you: the curve of the island, its gentle forest, its white sands. Look at the lagoon, whose colors melt at dusk to enter your heart, pleading with beauty, holding you captive to one single irretrievable moment. Look within, and listen to the child who sings so quietly, who is not the land child of thoughts or plans or desires, but who is the child of that same pleading beauty, merely asking to be allowed passage into the world. That child will not hinder or encumber you, because it has its own allotted place, it knows where it belongs. It will have its home wherever there is beauty, and will thrive wherever there is love. And for this you will love it freely and gladly.

Lucy presses her palms together, pressing hard in the pain of joy, in the liberation of understanding. All around her the signs confirm what she has understood. Through her tears the lagoon sparkles. And on the boat Robin is waving, a friendly greeting. He is surprised to see how she springs to her feet, how quickly she runs to the dinghy. He does not know how much she has to tell him, how already the light is fading, and that joy is a thing to be shared, quickly, without hesitation.

$\mathcal{T}$here it is, now, the sound of their engine, insistent and regular. It has woken me and they are leaving. The storm-scrubbed dawn is made poignant by their parting. I shall miss the adventure of the days in their company; I must be reapprenticed to solitude.

In a small pile on the beach I found tools, almost forgotten tools; some useless, some precious. Screwdrivers, knives, a small saw. A hammer—the coconuts are like butter to open now. I found what must be some sort of lighter, with a bottle of fuel and instructions which I read religiously. I found matches, which may only last until the next rain, unless I eat the jam quickly—then I can keep them in the jar for a time. Some clothing—simple jersey shirts, some sports shorts—what luxury! Needles, and thread, and scissors—now I shall cut my hair, to know that lightness and freedom again. And cans of fruit and vegetables with the can opener! And books, many many books, which make me blush at my theft, but also glad of it, for that way they learned that I could read, and English at that. Now I have Dickens and Shakespeare, Emily Brontë and Joseph Conrad, and a volume of poetry, and some Melville and Stevenson and even old Robinson Crusoe . . . I wonder what I shall make of that.

Yet I am afraid the books will make me long once again for human society, when I have learned at such a cost to be free of people and their strange ways. Or perhaps I will come to understand my good fortune, to be so bound to Nature and untethered by time; they know so little of this.

By the lagoon I sit in the crook of my favorite tree trunk; they could see me, if they cared to look this way. I am no longer afraid of decisions or discovery. I stay; they leave, taking with them a precious gift. For I witnessed the moment of telling—his joy, her serenity of acceptance.

Their departure happens almost too quickly for my eyes unused to change and evolution. One minute they are on deck, leaning over the anchor chain, cranking the handle of the windlass; the next minute the boat has turned her nose from me and is heading towards the pass. I read clearly her name upon the stern, a last footnote of irony to my story. Her flag flutters in the dawn breeze.

The girl Lucy is at the wheel, piloting her boat as once I piloted the plane. Her husband tidies things on deck, stopping now and again to hold her, to kiss her. Her face is upturned, open and receptive. I remember what that was like; I no longer know if my sadness at their departure is for them or for my past. They have found the meaning of kisses again. They are happy.

Quickly, almost imperceptibly, they are safely through the pass, gone into the wide world, so swiftly. Are they aware of the significance of that passage?

The white sails rise like plumes against the sky; the boat heels to the embrace of the wind, throwing great bursts of spray into the air like a colt let loose in a spring meadow. A frigate bird, eager for passage, circles the mizzenmast to look for a perch. To have wings and yet to want to ride . . .

I get to my feet and walk to water's edge. The girl Lucy is standing at the stern, something black held to her eyes, something which catches the sun, sending a shard of light to me. I wave, I smile—she has seen me through the ship's glasses. Her arm describes a hesitant circle against the blue. She alone has seen this strange ageless hermit at the boundary of her domain. Will she tell the world what she saw? Does she know, or even care?

I watch for a long time the slow progress of the boat on its course for the other, inhabited, islands. Each element fades gradually: first the name on the stern, then the crew, then the white hull, lost below the crests of the waves. For a long time I watch the three sails until they blend to two, then one, then none, over the horizon.

*O*n I fly, condemned.

The shadow of the plane shatters against the islands and is lost in their thick foliage. Only against the smooth sea does my shadow appear as I fly into the sun; only on the smooth sea could I ever land.

I did land there once; the tide took me to an island of love and pain which tried to keep me captive with memory. But I escaped and returned to my airy realm of clouds and dreams, released from the burden of remembrance.

In this place I am not alone; I share the baking cockpit with my navigator. I do not know him well; how strange to circle the earth like this, on and on, with a stranger. But his presence reassures me; he knows the way. He leads me safely through the endless confusion of islands, into history.

Once, as we flew low over a small bay ringed with a verdant thickness of hills, he shouted to me to look below. In a corner of the bay I saw a sailboat, her two masts brilliant white against the blue. From her deck a man, a woman and a small child waved, and their smiles and laughter rose to me upon the warm air. I dipped my wings in greeting, then they were gone.

They visit me sometimes, in dreams.

ACKNOWLEDGMENTS

This is a work of fiction; all the characters depicted herein are imaginary. However, the story which may be said to precede the events in my tale is firmly rooted in fact up to July 2, 1937, when Amelia Earhart and Fred Noonan disappeared, forever, on their flight from Lae, New Guinea, to Howland Island.

For the inspiration provided by that factual background I am deeply indebted to Mary Lovell's excellent biography, *The Sound of Wings*, and to Earhart's own *Last Flight* for many poignant details. For the more extravagant Earhart disappearance theories, readers may look into Fred Goerner's *The Search for Amelia Earhart* and *Lost Star: The Search for Amelia Earhart* by Randall Brink. My own tale does not in any way attempt to establish or suggest what happened to Earhart and Noonan—if indeed the woman on the island is Earhart. That I leave up to the reader to decide.

The reader will also search in vain for an island in Kiribati at 2°36'N, 174°10'E. I would, however, like to send my warmest thanks to Iataake King of the Kiribati Visitors Bureau for all the useful information about these little-known islands. The late Sir Arthur Grimble's *A Pattern of Islands* and *Return to the Islands* are a rich source for the folklore of the Gilberts' colonial period.

Many thanks also to Fred Glover of *Windflower* for the invaluable information about sailing in coral atolls, to Richard Curtis for his enthusiasm, to Gillian Blake for enlightening suggestions, to Mary Anna and Jo Ann for their encouragement and support, and to Alan for countless predawn mornings and long watches well beyond the call of duty.